The
Twelve
Steps

Zachary Crabtree

The Twelve Steps
By **Zachary Crabtree**

Published in association with:

Burning Bulb Publishing
P.O. Box 4721
Bridgeport, WV   26330-4721
www.BurningBulbPublishing.com

Edition ISBN

Paperback   978-0615581712

First edition.
Printed in the United States of America.

Library of Congress Control Number: 2011945696

Step 1

The headlights on the car were glowing in the rear view mirror of the Accord, smearing lights on the side mirror skirting the corner of Rudy's retinas and he was blinded. The car skidded five cars forward and the rear lights were smashed with the cover folded in the backseat. There were no passengers seated. Rudy was riding alone like a tiger prowling through the rain swatting the palms of trees, holding the steering wheel with wet paws and his arms fell over the steering wheel, his chest knocked the seat belt strap. He was flung back, the wheels scraping against the side parked cars, a minivan and a four-door sedan while the driver of the other car died in an instant when the seatbelt snapped and she flew against the windshield like a songbird flapping against a glass window, and in the passenger seat Diane was sloshing like a goldfish brushing her nose inside the bowl with a water cushion protecting her from the glass frame unawares her life companion had departed from this world, a shattered split second that would forever change her.

"Christine!" the words drawled from her lips as she awakened with a splitting headache when the paramedics were prying her from the automobile with the Jaws of Life. Diane was screaming at the bulk of her lungs and the shout rang in her ears, but she was barely whispering. Diane was struggling as if breaking from a restless sleep her body loaded in the ambulance while Chris was stiff, nearly wrapped in a dark cloud with a plastic sleeve.

Rudy was standing feebly in the street with a severe sense of vertigo, humming with a distraught feel of imbalance. He was walking towards the cars on the sidewalk that was tracing the rows of leaves with sharp points like the tip of a trowel. He was on the curb when the police wrote the report that he told with an honesty kin to disaster. He told the truth. There were times when the courts were soft. There were times he could walk. He had to serve a year.

Diane did not love Chris, at least not in the sense of the word that is thought of love, the physicality with passionate bodies touching however so briefly. Momentary tongues are closest the lovers ever came to true romance. Once Chris came to her crying. Diane did not bother to ask her. She did not say a word.

"If you do not come over here right this second and tell me what you are feeling!" Chris threatened an ultimatum, "then we are through!"

Christine had had a sexual liaison before she left work to come home. Although it was not the first time she strayed. She usually chose a time that would not confuse her when she was with her fiancé.

The image of her relationship came in short electric flashes same as an electric Tesla coil that curves like a spring with a blue spark. She was in and out of consciousness. Though she knew her lover was not faithful, she was in a constant slump of depression, stubborn denial of her predicament. The stage of the romance between the two torn lovers was a series of rented movies with the film clips edited with the reel skipping in-between clips.

Her first liaison was at the house where romance began, her home. The windows faded. The paint chipped from wood panels with a dogwood tree dropping leaves in spearing, blooming petals. Diane was tapping the glass pane while she was listening to the lovers thump lecherously on the misguided springs, and she wished the springs would cut into her back. Her decision to stay with the misguided romance was with the consciousness that her lover would not know that she knew, but as the years worn away the tired, dark charade, Christine was sternly aware while not wanting to tell Diane that she knew, too.

They were on different pages with a sugary alcohol disintegrating the ink. The pulse on the respirator counting the deterioration of Diane. All that made her who she was, her brainwave. The solid thump of her dead lover's heart in a caramel lump, sugary sweet is enclosing, unfurling, unloving and unmoving, so like their romance was the highway's steamy tar whereas driving vehicles weigh on the hardness.

"I did love her," Chris told her liaison. He made her promise not to tell Diane that she was with him, and he made her promise that she would tell Diane.

"If you ever are not true to our love, then we are through in a second," Diane told her fully knowing that she would never reveal her treason.

These incidences are lost with displacement in time and none of the love triangle points where the marks on the glass were. The suffering loss, gore, grotesqueness, Rudy finds himself drinking again. In Alcoholics Anonymous, Rudy is in a circle of trust with the pledges in the group, recalling his childhood and telling a story. He had told it many times before about when he was young and growing up. He was scrawny with vigorous challenges building muscles. The other kids would make jokes and he became obsessed with fitting in, not being seen as the odd man out. Here he usually would stop as it was confessional. Sometimes he would say that when he grew older, the stigma was not so difficult to take. The sting was still there and even if he could not be strong, he was safe with staying healthy, if not less handsome than when he was young. He relives when he took his first taste. Crawling upstairs as an alligator on all four legs under the bed sheets. When his father reclined on the mattress in a furling pose. He sipped his fathers' glass. The wine brushed his sweet palette with a bitter harshness. "Tell me about your father," the group leader Mike says.

"I live with my mother," Rudy says. "Should I talk about her?"

"Tell me this," Mike says. "There has been a burglar in your house, and some items of value have been stolen, jewelry, credit cards, so tell me your actions."

"I call the police. I check twice to see the stolen valuable and call the insurance company, and then file a report. I'd try not to arbitrate."

"A lot of gents came through there, didn't they?" Mike says.

"I have an interest in meeting," Rudy says.

"I need to clear out the dirty laundry," Mike says. He talks about romantic troubles with men. The last man he lived with and could not agree on basic household responsibilities. He asks the group to help him solve them.

Rudy's face was white with stiff, black hairs on his cheek and slicked, sweated hairs. The bald forehead was wrinkled with lines that showed age. He was older than the generation that did not belong, than the college pledges that were so young. He was not working and the unwholesome glimpse of the future sickened him to the core.

"He was a whore," Mike says. "I could not see that because I wanted the life my mother saw for me."

"I feel for you, Mike," Alex says.

"I wanted to live in a house with children," Mike says.

The sad sobbing of the group leader, Mike, was a beacon to Rudy's disambiguation, and he knew there was nothing he could take away from this meeting. He had five thousand dollars in the bank for a rainy day and the thunder and lightning had only been flashing for three months.

The traffic lights power was out and the cars came to a slow pulse, flowing like thick jam as the cab driver drove Rudy home. He wondered the limit on the charge the cab timer could clock while listening to the strange gypsy songs blasting through the sound-proof cab.

Boris was midday on a brick bayside path on the harbor and kicked a soccer ball into the aquatic waves, following the yellow streaks he made on the tan sky. The black and tan hues caught in a net of sky blue, until he saw not much further than the boats. He looked past the people walking towards him.   He saw into the past. His father was away until the weekend. Well into the day he was thinking about music school. He was not in attendance. He was hooking. The yellow and white colored adults did not block him his bright forwardness. He was slightly sun-burned and did not care to go inside for most of the daylight, but only on the neck, cheeks and forehead.   His arms were just beginning to sizzle under the sleeves of a jersey of the

Baltimore Blast. He was at an awkward stride, energy without hydration, and took notice of every sidelong glance, pause in his general direction, as if it were a deterrent to his goal. His goal was the barroom at a soccer ball that plot in the wave-curvature like light split with a cross-eyed stare rolling of the eyes. Piano glare, the sounds moved in colors-prismatic shades-rays bolstered on half bended heels. He was often a watcher of things, unobtrusively. Actual things that were all but ineffable to see as his science were quite naturally to see colors in sound and shape. The masses sunk, slipped by him, and him, them. He was caught up in the sun high above the plankton water, inland with gravitation balled in a tightly wound fist. There was a loud chorale as he went in, the drinkers were curtailing with loudly told bawdy jokes. He, a prism. "I'll have a negro modelo."

"One tall one, coming up," the bartender said. He was a whiskered Ukrainian with long teeth, and there was a feeling the mariners had had a bout with him. He had pale, sour cologne with heavy aftershave. He used a flowery deodorant and had tight pants, floppy belly hung on a belt loop with no belt. He was American to the teeth with a wisp accent slighter than the shade of his gray dyed hair, a shade lighter than black, but not black.

Boris felt like a piglet getting a drink from him, although the bar was not a crowd. He sat short for his age, fifteen, because his heritage was *Absolute*. He was a sure-achiever. Had to grab his drinks faster because he might pose as seventeen as but not much older than twenty and eighteen was the cutting off point.

"The balls of her tits," a man with boyish hair cut in the shape of a bowl, he said to end a discussion on his dick's embargo. He could make them shake at the crowded table by the back. "How many hot girls did you have on your dick?"

"I had a beautiful flower," Boris said. "I can promise you that!" The statement provoked laughter from the table, whose revelers saw that young man with bronze features come in here for the past week. He had dark blue eyes, was thin. He possesses the weight of a full man. Nor was he a thing.

The barbed wit stung quickly. He felt found out. He slapped his hand on the bar and left no dollar, not a thing for a drink that was never poured. By the standing smoky men he was vertical with a spring to his kick; he gave to the dust. He had had water, was not a hanger-on like a thin, gin drinker, a loiterer by the street shops, a wino with a bucket or bootlegger that was selling. He never much cared for fruit cocktail, the ricochet words snatched at with vodka too stingy to sting grasped at by the heel. He hit the street after loud bright language staccato coughs. His legs curtail the sidewalk legato pounce over gutters. He usually liked to see how far he saw the grunge. On the pavement there was white paint. He could still smell the bay. He had a swagger to his walk. He was thirsty. In the light he could see a truck speeding in the right on Light Street. The left lane had a line of cars at the stop light. The truck sped faster. Boris out of his periphery saw a boy riding a bicycle. Actually, later, he could not recall if he even saw. It was almost like a sixth sense that he knew. His eyes had rolled over. He knew the boy was going to get it across. Boris took a step on the white line and waved at the trucker. The truck kept its' speed. He gave a start. Lost in the crowd crossing the intersection, jay-walked at the T section. He closed his eyes and made to move in front of the truck. He did not budge. He made as if to go across, hopped on the sidewalk, fell sideways into the automobiles' streak. The mad driver, angry as hell, too, sped to a stop at the line, and at the bicycles' wheels turned on an angle and rotating almost touching the rubber of the truck struck it blinded by the mirrors and the traffic in the left. The boy yells. Boris can hear, "please don't tell Pastor Dan!" balanced on his handle bars, "I'm riding without training wheels. I just don't like them!"

"Must be easy to write self-help books," the crossing guard thought before those school children, holding his red sign. He had thought of a how-to book he felt compelled more than most, a step-by-step on defeating terrorists in the ghettoes by irritated hooliganism. Laughing children swam passed him. He had a .22. Just a little under than five minutes had slipped by since he saw a truck zone by going less than forty miles in a fifteen zone. The kids do not get out until three. He must know-the truck driver. It must be later for him. Clutch caught on the gears and ground an ugly kind. His foot was stamped firmly on the gas accelerated like a mechanical bull outside the hair stylists'. The torn drivers' seat spilled cotton stuffed balls lifted off the solid steel where the floor mats dissolved with ware. His sharp metal boots. Window peaks a crack. The re-circulated air was hot. The fuel made a cough at awkward places the truck stalled. "If I could make this light, "the truck driver talked to the truck. "Fuck him." The clutch notched, just a few. There's some asshole standing in the middle of the street. Seems to be swaying drunk, high or something. Should just run him over. Today's too hot. The clutch cranked so the wheels grind. The rubber tires burn. He could see the fuck just staring at him and gave him the finger. What an ass! A black boy on a bicycle whose wheels rotated at a forty-five degree angle with the base of the truck's tires. He almost made me hit him.

He was excused early. He was a decimal above ninety nine point five Fahrenheit degrees. Washington Carver had an assistant principle telephone his parents. German rode his bicycle. The training wheels had come off. Exited the back of the building to unchain his bike, riding with a fever took the busiest route home, exhilarated and not all that sick. "I'm no Hutu, cows" he called with his lungs panting quarts of air. He was calling at the trucks which he called cows. The traffic lanes' became fields spotted with strange faces behind shields that all seemed to stop for him. The truck driver cursed beneath the wheel he saw as the bicycle slid beside the tires and jumped the curb. He saw a young man that helped him and was hollering, "I hope Pastor Dan doesn't know! I'm riding without my training wheels!"

He came home to an empty house. The coat rack in the vestibule hung slick raincoats on wood hooks. He could hear the sigh of the short piano in the adjoining room. The bourgeois piano was familiarly thought of as sacred. In the form stone house the furniture ached with wood sighs. The wooden pieces falling off the nails on the coat rack. On the furniture the bed sinking further to the floor. The floorboards cried with a wooden moan. Boris became livid. He grappled the neck of a contrabass with his hand on the bloated belly, like a woman, the F holes carved into the front board sang with echoes, reverberation as the metal lifted from the carpet, the metal in pin on the bottom of the bass stuck in the floor like a cane of an old woman's, which Boris walked with down the hall to bring the instrument to the end of the block, to wait for the bus to take him to the orchestra.

The brick houses row to row, form stone and brick: he saw houses lights which shown inhabitants lived in some. The broken houses, no one lived in, or near. He carried an instrument to the bus stop by the fixed and broken bricks. There was no one out at the sun down. He arched himself to keep the frame from touching the asphalt. Legs gave large gaps between feet. Unspeaking, how to get on the bus was a difficult request made to the bus driver and the passengers. He leaned the neck beneath an arch in the sliding door. He lifted the wide hips to fit snugly between the narrow passages. After he squeezed by a ticket-taker machine and paid his fare, Boris took a seat in the front of the bus. An old lady and a commuter stood and made to stand off.

"You're falling asleep, I don't want to mean you'll miss your stop," the guy on the other seat said. The metal floor shook and so did the strings beneath his prints. He could hear a fanfare in the orchestra before taking a spot on the stage.

"I don't subscribe to your beliefs," Boris said. "What?"

"You're dreamer," he said "rerouted to Latin America, Brazil" to work at a job the government laid out for him in the country's poorest ghetto, the double bass man had to see a guy on the other seat down the block in his travels, which was a coincidence to be on the same street across the continent and have someone seated so close, live so close-by. He preferred his women ogling from far away. "It's her.   I'm dreaming her," Boris said. "She was the younger."

"What did she do?" the guy asked.

The guy looked on intently, and really Boris felt no need to hold back, he had realized all his misgivings, and the man looking on had the kind of face a mother would appreciate. "My name's Jim," Jim said.   "Hey Harold," he said to Harry slouched seated beside him.

"She confessed to me her deepest secrets when I was young.   I told her my junk," Boris said.   "I had an argument with her," Boris said.   "We were living together in the suburbs; I was missing when she worked all day. I saw an episode on the television set about a film maker wakes up and makes loves to his wife, and sleeps through the whole thing!"

Jim became interested suddenly as the double bass player seated across from him read the street signs that appeared in the tinted glass window between him and Harold.

"Greta woke me up and did the same thing, and it drove me crazy," Boris said. "The next day, she woke me up again, and that time I slept through the whole thing. She says to me afterwards, 'If you don't know any better, that was rape.' I was about to give her a smack for the joke, but she was dead serious. I denied it, of course, but later had to admit. You know I wish I had taken myself under better care, but I still don't know whom to believe."

"Were you married?" Jim asked. Boris shook his head and the frame of his instrument jostled out of sync.

He sent a request by telemarketer on a mobile phone. She told him an offer with special deals in the form of magazines. All he had to do was give his land line. The stage at the Orchestra at a thought resembled the international phone on a street corner in Milan. He sent a message to an answering machine on his parents' line. That walk he took at night in Milan was feverish. The air was hot. In his hands he held his girl's hand, which felt lukewarm. They sat in a playground at the city park beneath the canvas of trees on dirt roads, and the fountain at the Piazza. The horns exploded with violets colors and oboes sang Stravinsky's line in pinks fizzled sunbursts like the fire sticks on July fourth.

The wave of umber hues rose out of the violins. He saw rays across the cello. After the conductor's stick broke through like a hand moving beneath the water. Greta had sores on her feet and she blamed him for them. He rubbed her foot in water in the bidet at the Milan Hotel. Later they fell asleep on the comforter. Breakfast buffet in the basement with the room full of mirrors, she took yoghurt and he had cereal, where in the 2% milk flakes floated in a pattern foretold his future with her.

He started missing notes and blamed his fingers. He was caught on scrap booking, the wash towels in the hotel bathroom in his suitcase that are in his washroom, as the dead skin rubbing in the grooves of the double bass strings. "He's your Uncle, not your dad, he's the best friend you ever had," James said. A walk in the Robert E. Lee Park the hooligans tip-toed barefoot on the dam across the lake. Her feet in the water seemed to slipup. His brain wandered to the flakes floating in the milk.

He began talking to himself in a silent dialogue. "Excuse me," the contrabass always took his time before bed to pee. He almost fell asleep on the shoulders of his bass. "The tests are back, and we've allocated the results," the operator spoke on her mobile. Her urgency was punctuated with a jab. The orchestra continued to play Rachmaninoff before the silences. "Don't sugar coat me," Arty said. "You have SIDS," she said. "I wouldn't interrupt this unless it were important," Arty said hand-lifted-over the receiver and a bass neck leaning on his shoulder, strings reverberated with violence.

"There is a tumor behind your left ear," the operator spilled out. He could hear. "Excuse me, a second. I need to tell the conductor something. He's waving. You can't stop." He covers the receiver with deep breathing. There is a bow marked by an upside down carrot on the second note in a series on the part. He can elbow the note with an accented swing. "What is your insurance number?" They were just numbers too blurry to read. He had an insurance card. His fingers trembling. He held himself the best he could on the shoulders "Cancer," Arty let out a frustrated sigh, "schizophrenia?" he asked. "What's your name?" The startled tubas let fall their horns, "Is there room for a contrabass?"

"My name is Cherry," Cherry said. His babbling went on. He was stuck on that note until seconds later the notes begun to accelerate in a low, rumbling ostinato. James shook his head and rather than explain himself took the section out for beers. "Thank God it's over finally, "Boris moved his lips to the sounds, breathing air to the vowels.

The basses lay in a row by side with the music stands, and the lights shone on the keys in a tin glow. The bass section crossed the road in a line of melancholy downcast shoulders and the group sat at a table away from the bar. Cologne made Boris' throat chafe, and he broke out in a rash. You're talking to yourself. Don't act like we can't tell," James said. Deidra lifted her magazine and held up a picture of a handsome, male model with a pose in a stoic embrace hugging an attractive young girl in a black slip.

"I've burned my nose on something, the aftershave on his tie," Boris said, blushing. The very thought enraged him. He had put up with her apish behavior, and told her to quit it. Her shyness became aggressive, then volatile. A few crumbs on the kitchen

16

countertop-and the haranguing did not cease until he left or she left, and neither did. He might just admit he's still not over her, and then James asked, "Whose Arty?"

"Arty?" Boris said surprised. "I knew him."

"I shouldn't ask?" James asked scratching a bruise on his leg. The basses sat at the bar for a drink before winding down. A short hour long lounge before the drive home with instruments in tow. "I should get going. I have a bus to catch before nine," Boris said, "and it won't wait."

"What went wrong?" James said, nudging at the bruise. "I told her," Boris said, "that I was kidnapped. I've never told anyone that, except her and you. It was embarrassing."

"Why did you do that?" James asked.

"She told me her secrets. In her pretty, dollish high teens she sold her naked body to a pornographer. The video aired on you porn until someone on the street recognizes her-needless to say, it was embarrassing. She was on the couch with some machine and an extendable phallus pushing a steel bar with a dildo into her vagina's gravitation."

"Some hippy," James said, "don't care about her; she don't care for you." A roast beef sandwich as tall as his knuckles was on a plate. "What used to be on the block was the plantation. It's hard to believe how some

17

things stay the same," he chewed. "North is south, and the south shall never rise!"

Arty was a choirboy when he was eight--just before turning ten years old, and he used to watch the television show Beverly Hills 90210 and after decide which one of the famous actresses he was going to marry by who had the most gross income per. Was it Shannon Doherty? The blonde? The brunette? In the 1990s he argued with a cop about a ticket instead of heading to traffic court, and he insulted him with insults. Pig. Pork. Fat and lazy. He sped away from tickets or cop cars. He was hounded un-relentlessly by Police until he was fatal. His Mercedes sped across the rim of the highway bending the sparks across the drivers' side; the airbag buried his head in his lap.

Rudy spied through the Plexiglas window. He enjoyed the sight of women. And to him, they really were girls. Small figures stretched in the glass came in closer between flexed electric slides opening the automated doors. His eyes were better up near the convenient store register. He disliked waiting in lines, and getting caught with his pants down. The line barely moved. He held a bag of groceries. His thick ankles, large calves and heavy thighs sturdy on feet wide like fanning fishes. Getting up was the worst, shoving ahead, wiggling the coccyx to the aching lumbar on the vertebrae of his lower back traveling in short charges to his middle. He got in the car and drove home fast.

His unemployment check came in the mail. His veterans' check was monthly, and could cover his expenses. His retirement assets were substantial enough to pay the plaintiff. He lived in squalor, but chartered bliss to him, to the prostitutes a place to work that night or day of the week. The phone rang.

"No, *no me degas*! You are a fish out of water, Rudy! I want you there at next weeks' meeting." It was Mike.

"I'm fine. I'll pay. Don't call here," Rudy said.

"I care, we care," Mike said.

"I can take care of myself, so take care of your own goddamn problem," Rudy said. Hung up the phone. "Faggot," he said in a churlish groan. He went for a drive in the Bay Place by the green hills with gravestones. The car made a stop abruptly at a cement marker. He fed a meter and pushed his ankles in the soil to surmount the heights. Steep, too steep for him. He drove his own face obfuscated in the mirror.

Margery put on her makeup at the mirror with the gold frame on her ellipsoidal features in an oval lining; she spent hours painting on her smooth skin, staring at her face with one applicator brushing her half-closed eyelid until she was painted blue, and rouge; her fat decorated with lace and string, and her dark hair combed a hundred motions over in tin shiny with hairspray curled over her. Her soft glow a scent of pomegranate perfume, grapefruit toiletries misted the natural sweat and hormones.

He had a wire tap on the phone line. It was not her -it was to satisfy his own curiosity he eavesdropped on her nightly conversations. But it was not just her. There was a wire tap on her neighbors' landline, and where the third wire was no one's business. Not even his.

Perhaps the too early departure of a loose one emboldened the endless obsessing by the mirror over her toiletries. When he was on the street he stared at the cement. He had a curly beard, and dark eyes that no one knew the true color to. A scrapped applicator in her trash became a clue into her rich palette. She was pregnant. If even the ricochet of pebbles under his foot did not strike him now how they flew than pretty soon he would obsess over that too.

Boris came home after the rehearsal and to his room put his bass slantwise on the corner post of his bed. A hat topped the pole in the shape of a bell that curves outwards woven from plaid fabric by the feel of the course hair seemed to be wool. A cardboard box had donations for the homeless in sweaters worn to the thread that had yet to be unraveled, a few objects of canned goods and a rolled up poster of Groucho Marx posing with a cigar between his comedy faux, yet actual, rather large teeth. A chalk Buddha decorated with felt fabric pieces cut into a red nose, purple ears and seaweed, lemon and cherry squares thread to look like a clown's face, sat stationary across from the bed sheets tossed freely on the laminate-less pine floor beside the mattress. The springs sank with the weight of Boris' lower posterior. He could feel the quilts on the blue, bare cushioning dig in him and the foot of the bed frame shake on the wood. Dolly said to her husband, "Go to the store to pick up some milk. See that the cat is fed," in the kitchen adjacent to her son's room. Her husband, also Boris, came to the door and knocked on the frame. "I'll send Boris out and see that the cat is fed!" His wife Katija, Dolly was a pet name for her, as was the cat also a cute thing he called her, wanted her husband to do something. Boris junior could hear in her voice, as well as see.

"This coffee is bitter," his father, Boris said after a sip in a shallow cup, "was it just put on?"

"The coffee taste fine," his son Boris junior said, although he never called him that, just son, "the grounds are fine grains." He rolled the course coffee with his tongue savoring the bitter, sandpapery flavor.

"I have to tell you, I ground something in with the beans, son" Boris said. "You should not be alarmed. It's called Fluoxetine. The effects are not immediate and you shouldn't notice any difference in sleep schedule yet. It's a mood enhancement drug. The doctor thinks it should help with your problem if you keep taking the pills, and I want you to."

Boris swallowed the grounds and saw in his cup an oily pattern, shapeless, had a grainy glare on the liquid. He stood up too fast and the pressure dropped to his knees. He was dizzy. "I'm not mad," Boris said. "Seems you've been bothered by this for a long time," Papa said. "Was the timing wrong? You lost her," Boris' father had to clear his throat. He had cut back on cigarettes to one pack a day, and had to take out a cigarette to spark before reminding his son, "your friend died soon after. You never told me. I had to tell you."

"I don't mind the pills, it's just sometimes I feel like I'm being flanked by wild horses," he said. "She was chasing some idiot around a pool to suck him off, papa, and I didn't care. He had his third abortion that year, and never used a condom, and she was angry with me because that stupid hick blamed me." Boris' son stared at the whitewash and told his papa this, and refused to blink. The chagrin on her pregnant face sank into his eye like a slideshow in the dark. She did not want to be a mother-she never did. Her uterus had begun to swell and her body was showing.

"Fluoxetine makes you alert, or sleepy, and you should have diarrhea at first, but that goes away with a week's dosage," papa said. "If it's too much, take the pills." Boris' father had no answer for his son's predicament. He knew his mother would be sad to hear the words escaping her sons' lips. So he unbuckled his belt and lifted the leather strap out of the loop. Boris crawled over on his side, and Boris senior gave a thwack. The strap snapped just under his shirt and left a

22

red sore. The wound however minor wasn't aggravated by the sting of the buckle.

He held his breath. Before his eyes was a streak of red, which faded after he began to breath. "I did something good today," Boris told his father. "I saved a boy's life."

"Don't lie to me, son," Boris' father spoke. He was less grave re-looping his belt, and clasping the buckle to his khakis. He shook the floor with his red loafers. The boards rumbled like elephants' mating.

"I saw a lady's smile and swear I smelt him riding on his bicycle a few blocks down the street before the busy road before I stumbled on the street in front of the truck speeding towards him and me. I might have signaled to the boy first," Boris admitted. "It might have been my fault he did not stop at the corner before the light. The light was about to go red. The truck driver was not going to stop," Boris caught his breath. "But he might have. I can't tell now, I just went blank, and it's a blur. I was standing right in front of the trucks' grill, but it might have been the headlights. There's no way of knowing if I would have lost one, or both legs. Or I might have died with a snapped spine, in just a split second like a snap."

"How did you and Arty meet?" Boris' father asked. He had read an email James wrote about Boris' friend, concerned his alternate in the higher register of the contrabass had dissolved his sanity like razing hairs on

23

the head. Unlike Boris who never liked to wet his hair, except with soap to dilute the wetness with a protective sheer-his superstition that wetness washes the vitamins out, and testosterone soaks in after washed hair loses wetness. James ran a wet comb through his few hairs at the break of dawn religiously. "What in God's name was running through you?" Papa asked his son. "Did your short life flash before your eyes. Did you think you were going to die?"

"I saw myself standing on the top of a stairwell in the dark, and there was a light at the bottom, and so I jumped off the top step to the strip of light like racing through time in white, panel wood stairs; several seconds passed where I could not see the spacing of a door, and then the door was open. I was never falling, and until recently, not much has been happening. Things have been slow always falling deliberately," Boris said, "I did not want anyone to think what I did was deliberate, that it," he unintentionally made an ugly frown on his eyebrows, "was suicide. I sat across from Arty in the chorus. I saw how his expression changed before he went and he saw me. Like it was I the only one who noticed. Everyone said he was going to go, but I knew."

"You cannot carry the guilt with you," Boris said, "you are much too romantic." It was true Boris was as blind in love as he was romantic to the point of vulgarity. Blind to all except for his nose, and his nerves to be touched, or untouched by the music of the cars and the street, as by the gospel lull of a choirgirl. He took communion, drank wine, ate the bread, and Arty kept the bread held under his tongue to stow in his locker later with his robes and medals. His father kept his son in a room with Queen sized beds, and the bric-a-brac collected from about his small mansion. On the weeks where choir practice began too early to drive from where Boris' family lived, Arthur and Boris slept in a two bed room. Arty swept under the covers, the sheets pulled tightly over his chin which he pulled off frustrated because he enjoyed the act of masturbation in Boris' company only. For awhile his friend watched him, and said nothing. The two boys stripped bare naked laid on the antique carpet floors, as Arthur groped a manikin with its bikini top disrobed from her and with hard laughter though he could not see in the dark its polyester b-cups stared at Boris' member hardened on the tan felt and then at the floral design on the bra strewn across the floor by the quilted bedspread which formerly had his member. They had parents' eyes on them in the church. Except when to put things in the locker after singing morning mass the choirmaster had his hands in Arthur's pants.

On the playground was the last Boris knew of Arthur, who for years had kept the secret from the other choirboys. Suddenly a football hit him in the glasses on his nose, which falling from his face landed away a few feet. He had his hands on his nose to check for bleeding. His eyelids were glued shut. The table in physics class the teacher tapped on. The test answers were underneath the desk beside Boris' desk, and Arty placed them so Boris may be tempted. The answers were hard to grasp but he tried and was caught not cheating. "Who put these here?"

"I'm not going to ask you how you're doing," Pierre said to German when he was home from George Washington Carver Elementary on that day he came to a close end, a truck on the wheels of his bicycle.

"Someone saw me," German said. "I told him not to tell!" To him his father was more than the world, and the words of a Pastor were solid gold. There was no shame for him knowing his father Pierre refused to earn a license to drive, and rode everywhere on the bus. In fact, it brought him great pride that his father along with the tribal leaders chose public transportation as an act of boycott against discriminatory practices against people belonging to their community, so that all shared the same reprimand for a traffic officer's bullying of the groups' Pastor Dan, as he liked to be called. His pseudonym was of the Spanish, they give.

The heater coughed, and Pierre lifted the latch of the metal hood. The hinge creaked. He banged the machine until the coughing smoothed to a hum. Ota polished the cedar living room table with lemon scent Lysol and her little brother crawled on the wet surface, then fell on his back off the edge on the rug. The plate glass window curtained behind the set beige drapes and the cling of the static on the black monitor seemed to draw the negative polarities. Ota enjoyed looking at plants, and things that reminded her of nature. She sat longingly on city park benches to see birds and trees. Her joys at the harbor smelling the salty bay water. The sight of the jostling waves exhilarated her. Pierre had thin layers of scalp wax, and she cut hers short above her shoulders, tiny wisps of coarse blackness and ebony, oblong temples marked with Caucasian scars beneath the pigment of her skin, old wounds healed into her, her long voyage to the town to meet her father was miraculous.

He knew he could not call the cops. Pierre said finally, "it was because of our Pastor, not what you did. He refused to let him be, and the man felt bothered."

"He drove faster, and I was blindsided by a car and a traffic pole," German said. "I knew it was my problem, not his."

"Listen to your elders because they know the secret to getting older, and you will not get younger. If you know this single bleep of their time is a century's worth of theirs, which you may never return," Pierre said. "Always return your school library books, and never keep an overdue slip if you can recess the fine." He had numerous examples to hand his son, like a missionary to the boy hands a dollar and lets the bill slip from his fingers. He had three children. To him that was a fortune.

"There was an accident, and a student tried to step in front of a car. Lucky for me he was there," German said. "The truck might not have, and I might not be here. He seemed sad before he did it, like he was getting away from someone."

"I count my blessings," Pierre said. "I should be so lucky to have fortunate things happen for my children," and shortly after a brick shattered the plate glass crashed under the table and the pieces fell flatly behind the cabinet.

Step 2

Boris' shrill hums in class were a distraction to the students and as for himself Rachmaninoff piano scales leaped like antelopes in his eye. He was a frolicking hunter for the gazelle's horns, where striped swallows wail on bleached savannahs. Their songs had resounded him an entire hour. He was caught on the tune at sun up, and he became entirely immersed with the imitable incantation. A hat had the seams fold inwardly with his book sack. His school supplies were distingue. Seams outward as the lines on a map define a new border to a state like the Mexican line with Guatemala resembles the shape of Texas standing on its hands upside down also seemed to him a Spaniards' attire to the special girl he admires. His attempt was to seem Parisian. He thought of her as classy, and no one else was quite like her, except for her little sisters' twelve years younger than she. And to her siblings he forgot to take a book of Terry Southern short stories at her apartment above her parents' house which was later there for her younger sisters to preamble.

"The neighbor cut the rubber stopper on my windshield wipers," Boris said to her. "He's such a stupid fuck. I drove by my fathers' diesel engine, yet to blame my neighbor is an argument against his daughter. She has inherited of his anger."

Lizzie gave a surprised stare, as she was discussing some controversy with Deidra she heard just recently on the radiophone. She thought the violence was a computer error, that it somehow did not belong to her place to give way.

"I was feeling angry," Boris said. "At him, at me, at my neighbor…"

"Denis Quaid's wife gave birth to twins," Deidra said. "At the hospital a nurse gave shots of blood thinner that was meant for someone else's babies."

"Did the babies die?" Boris asked. "And why was it his wife's twins, and not someone else's babies?" He doubted the coincidence and likewise tossed his inquiry on toast points to the steaming virtue.

"A computer error did it. See. No one is to blame," Lizzie interjected, but the connection Boris' reasoning was long complicated by fiscal responsiveness. If it was because of him. It tormented a moral sentiment to always be kind to the neighbor. Dennis Quaid was a famous movie star to Boris as the serf to a servant of the Czar's, as in, he knew the actor by reputation, the worker feel felt for the movie house. So if Boris so much as coalesced with the wrong gentleman on the street, the neighbor was vengeful. He knew the block had a way to understand things in cohesiveness, and that one line of yarn became unglued meant himself bled in an innocuous spool. His brain was wired to feed from rivers and locks that feel thinner with blood flow, bleeding aware the way it fed a superstition. "Excuse me," Boris said to Deidra and Lizzie. She kept her controversial lines radioed in on the phone while Boris went to the lavatory to go. He fed the mouth of the rivers. The pegs on the bass and the screws on the bridge. He tightened with the fear the wood might crack, and if the varnish cracked, nothing protected the bass except for layers, eventually layered thicker than the instrument. To have the strings tight, and screw the pegs on the bridge, he might raise the strings such the fibers did not rattle against the fingerboard anymore. But that may break a string.

He did not go to defecate in the bowl, wash his hands in the sink and towel off, but to escape out of the window in the bathroom to the school playground by the street fence where Boris met his old classmate Arty on the field while both kept eyes and ears out for cars. His bass was in the closet in the band room which he'd fetch when he saw the steel tops of the Volvo Margery had swiped from her fathers' garage. Fumes blew smoke from the cigarette in Arthur's cool hands. Boris never had a cigarette.

"Lizzie is the perfect Catherine Deneuve in a pink sweater," Boris said. "Her blue eyes are cool and her long hair is blond to a fine point. Her ends have been cut with tweezers. But Deidra," he said. "Is a hot brunette who dyes her hair black, looks like she is careless with her combing. Her butt ripens smoothly, flatly I'd suckle like a fat calf." He breathed in the carbons that fumed out of Arthur's mouth.

"Boar," Arthur said and as Boris lifted his head he got kicked in the scrotum with his friends' sneakers. "Never mention ever what happened between us, or else." Boris collapsed to the grass and clutched at his balls with clasped hands he'd hold at night feeling for the dislodged bowl-shaped lumps, secretly fearing cancer or worse. He saw colors fade to yellow like electric candlelight. Then dots floated before him, a miasma on the dirt like a hallucinatory grasshopper hops in the tall green shards broke off glass. He was hurt most by Arthur's shoes. The frustrated feeling he had something Boris never could have. Only working harder, had he the thirst. His friend said that to him in actions, but the very last time they spoke Boris said plainly to him that, "God is dead, and you have to believe that you were wrong." The sting of lying clicked loudly clutching to the sharp points on his poised spine. "Do you mind turning your cheek," Boris said. Arty did. He smacked him in the nose in the bone clung fast to the fatty cartilage dislodged it from Arthur's face. "Don't mention this again, or else," Boris said. Beneath his nose, eyes bruise. "You were

32

the fatted calf," Arty told him. "No," Boris said, and slapped his bone loosely. They never spoke again.

The Swedish Volvo was blue with a white hood peeking over the line of cars on the street like a snowcap after the brand of chocolates with a frosted coat. The bass had to be stored in the musicians' closet for at least that night, and the next two days before Boris had a chance to retrieve his stand-up instrument. Arty saw in the front seat with Margery in the drivers' seat and Boris in the backseat with a box of used clothes bought from a second hand store beside a girl named Zoë. She wore fishnet stockings. He recognized the highway stretch by the pale yellow of the grass on the fields. Boris always looked at his fingers as he had things in his hands, at where the tendons flexed to the cringe in his forearms. He stared at his hand at the thought of retrieving three dollars he had saved for ducking out of school before the bell. "Why don't we stop at the Dunkin Donuts?" Boris asked Margie in the drivers' seat, "because I'm lost," she said turning slowly on an off ramp. "Somewhere near the airport," she said clutching the brake as a fast Jeep ran right through a line of baby ducklings. "It was not love," Boris said.

"It was not love what?" Margie asked breaking her hand at the knob on the clutch. He was to marry. He was someone who loved. She knew how to get what she wanted and could only say how to get things in that way she wanted; she could have no other way to get her point across better. He could do no better.

"Those that love you must keep, keep you from the unkept things to quarry yourself," Boris in the car as they went down from the beltway loop. "You'd got a duck," Zoë texted on a blackberry-a hyperawareness to sudden viruses, a flash of awareness to hypertexts and a textual awareness to mundane personalities, a novelty to some was her black book, which had to entertain a novel enough bricks to build a textile mill. Her forwarded movie pics had enough textiles to pack a bill on a Carnival Cruise whose sign advertised. The .bic was incompatible to her unmentionables. Her bra adjusted. It was her favorite. They drove, the Prince of Egypt Jewelers went by. The latest advertisements at the bus strops' were for the Cruise liners. Travel frightened her.

At the Donuts went by an African girl with a knitted hat, and Margie asked for directions, bought a large coffee with non-fat dairy creamer and a glazed doughnut. Her words are free as her tongue sipped a hot beverage. Her boyfriend saw her in his heterotopic brain smear as gray matter in his ear, which is found lacking in her, scarred her like a boiling pot tossed over the side to keep her his. He said to her, "she can own his words, love is a whisper we cannot know." A boy to her in a phrase was, what begins as a guide undeveloped boys becomes a summer camp.

As Boris took a bite of an applesauce doughnut and the car drove, his ex-girls short porn star career. Was *James and The Giant Peach* who wanted to dig in to peaches, to get the soft fruit dripping or like a duck quacks always there's quacking to go by to see where the duck has gone, where the duck had waddled through to get where he was. Zoë scribbled E-novelettes on her arms like music playlists. He cut up fed to her of his illegible script indigestible in big bites as baby sauce is. Crushed apples spooned with tiny silver, the peelings, the lead spoon which is in her hands on her portable wireless phone and in the fish is Iodine squirming in a juice, a liter of white wine vinaigrette at the wheel, she led, as the pop star says, have you ever, ever. The Dickens club: Dick-ins, a play on book ends of a sort of semi-club. The fish de-boned with the forked head stared with gross, milky eyeballs. He fell for her, he fell madly for her, and she tossed the skin. He rolled his eyes, and the bend of the pop song leaking out the stereo was palpable, but vanished at the thought of his string contrabass in the closet put to a knife, carved in the varnish the sign of a hooligan punk. They drove by a trend setter The Zone closed for as long as he knew. Abandoned in a house, unfed dogs clawing scratches on his perfectly varnished laminate instrument which wore in the dark. Boris' eyes recognized all the shades of light of all the hours of the day, little nuances of a musicians' life, brush teeth-hand movements-raking leaves. His joys urge her to suffer, her illness, her feelings and her wellness kills her, because she gives it up for his. Her needs to him happiness. The girls made of sweet, candied liquor. The girls out of whores. Her mother put up with it. Margie has a gloomy look for fame, a squib, jabs cut paper butterflies, low-light files. Nail polish remover, a childhood wasted through fumes. Her pink flesh paint pots had candy stripes.

He had delicate hands, the kind that work hard to snap the lids off glass jars, his joints squeezed only to touch metal like holding an orange soft to the feel, slipped pressure before giving. He wanted to break a dent. "There is no black and Jew," the anglophile Boris said, "I am Tandem!"

"We know as woman a black Jew," Margie said eyeing the passing motorists for a spot to change lanes to the accelerating tractor trailer in the left lane, signaled to before the angry squeal of breaks began choking the truck to an even grind.

"There is no we as women because there are no collective women unconsciously. You," Boris said. "You, you are womankind like there is mankind. If all the women came in one massive orgy, there'd only be pigs rolling in their own mud. I've said it," Boris said. She looked in the mirror of a girl whose face was bathed in fire.

"Your of the generation of the fifties, should've lived in the twenties," Margie said. "You Jews don't know your own blues."

"My father's no Jew, my mother. I'm no Jew. Jew sand blacks, or your mother's a Jew of the twenties, get with the nineties," Boris argued as the Volvo was changing lanes, the lights of passing motorists shined on the slowing wagon.

"You learn your mothers' racism, and your own chauvinisms," Margie threw the big words.

"I've heard it three ways, and it's always some straggler of the boonies comes to this town to get laid by the KKK," Boris said. "Shouldn't have lived nothing. Never should've been given birth to me, my mother!" He argued with her habitually. They took a route to the lawns of strangers houses in hot resale markets at odd hours. "Stop being so conceited," she said, "and who was looking at you, her straw blonde hair. You were looking too like she was a Finn, blonde bomb!"

"I was," he said even the ice blue of her eyes stained him like a spilled soda in a movie theater. "You blame me, but I am a tired man. Girls so stupid even an old man's touch scares, or as Arty says he goes to a corn field with an automatic to shoot at the skies," he argued once to her in the middle of the night so late, the early morning routines of the neighbors had all but just begun. "Danny Devito in an inflated flight suit had

37

broken the seal to suck crystallized piss in a straw, sort of like cereal if it was chewed before swallowed in the roof of the mouth, shaped like a springy tube like those found in teeter tots, the sound when sprung like a trunk, or astronauts suck oxygen attached to tanks with compressed CO_2," Boris said about the dream he had woken from that morning, "And then on my head we had forgotten to remove the yarmulke on my hat borrowed in synagogue the school brought us to, to pray which Arty stood before the torah shouting like a kid whose bottle was impossible to get."

The worse was Arty who borrowed his uncles' SUV and drove drunk and woke the neighbors of houses he had never been to with the crashing of his front end into their newly painted BMW, so dark he did only see the sparks in the pitch black as he hit and ran the motor to the next furthest neighbors' block on a binge he took during the worst hours. The darkest night owl had nodded off to be heckled awake by the commotion, the shouting hectic awoke the neighbors, as did the crashing.

"Why celebrities?" Margie eventually asked Boris, as the blue rectangular wagon drove on the street of a hooligan who was recovering. In the garage Lonny held a metering rod he struck the sides of with a wired metal tube which made the metal cling, and scrape. The resin charred on the wires with the rod letting the cold, black ash loose. He had made a bong out of the thing.

Lonny's mother hobbled in the room with her one diabetic foot to fold his laundry in a basket in the basement as her son hung off the rickety, chair legs rattling on the pavement. She went through the garage sidestep. His arms shook like a skeletons' with arm tattoos blazing with the ink still hot flowers and skull heads. His mother did not skulk. She drew a caring sidelong look of the four after school guests who took to her son like houseplants.

Mike N' Ike stares in the toilet bowl reflection. He ponders the filth and grime. He could still smell the shit on his hands. The bathroom soap dispenser had a thin pinkness stuck to the bottom of the bottle. He grasped the doorknob. He walked with his gaze on a sheet of black ice with a look he focused hard to see beyond the glare covering the walk of every aspect of his being. Diane saw him through her glass at the table. She had her egg sandwich and was sensitive to his germs.

He made an empty gesture at a motorist on his way to the Steak N' Eggs. Diane's smile wanted him to smile also. Mike N' Ike waved her off, "hello," he said to her shaking all five fingers of his hand loosely detached his ring finger. Looking for the car he saw the driver who was with her young daughter as if he should offer an apology to her for attempting to cripple him. Diane said, "I want you to smile." Her fear was socializing gave her a chance to be a heroine. He squeezes a sliver of ketchup to dress a fry. He dresses each fry on the plate before eating, putting down the ketchup bottle between fries on the placemat, and when she looks at him, he dresses on a fry twice tangentially yet ignoring her. Mike N' Ike spills some coke on his fry. Mike N' Ike hears her vaguely seems to notice as she got up walks past to the storeowner to complain about the smell like socializing was a disease we are racing for the cure. He checks on her temperament. Diane boils. She sped ahead no one saw her ever since.

She held the phone in her hand, that thing used most to communicate, the hands were vitals she spoke with for her heart. Sometimes she could not. Her emails had no reply sent. She sat by the phone, a ghost waiting for her lover to tell, to call her. She had his name. She he expected to hear from a joke. He was lopsided to him entering a building. She never joked. The seriousness overwhelmed them. He never did apologize. Her grudge outlasted them. She had nightmares of her sitting outside her house in a car with a lipstick lighter, a cigarette. She read the case history at her desk. The bread winner never was a guardian. He let people feed on him like pigeons kicked in the street. He saw dogs as kinds of rats. His son never understood. A fecund household he'd come home to everyday after he'd walk all the places he needed to be. On an evening he'd start to kick the wall fixture until it came loose. Setting him off was an easy thing to do. She had one more house visit. He said he had a knife. His hand something in his trench coat on the bus. "Why we send some children home. I can't talk about things you've done because you'll never be any different," Diane said to herself. She saw his nude figure in the afternoon slouching in bed (camera to the window shade snapshot picture plates). "People stop shouting at night," she said, "masturbation was bad for the asshole, who's at fault. He knew he was. He must be dangerous to himself," she thought contemplating who he was, the file said he claimed to be a nudist last she was at 1706.

He dropped by the stoop. Margie sped off while profanities strung out the window threw like tapping gently on a pane of glass tossing a paper Dixie cup in a gutter out a moving car her dress at her foot clinging to her knee, her non scent Boris never could slake. The breath mint addiction to chew a tin, full tins in the entirety. He kept the empties souvenirs to her taste. He was made servile with a limp. He was crushed. He fell for her and the heart thickened to a sickening syrup flow in a heartbeat. He was tired. Boris never could. Walked in thick traffic cars stalled as he cut through. The sheen of a hair shedding in the glimpse of the dark by the by. He had to drain a leak in the radiator stunk of ammonia. The string on his glimpse of a hair. 1% of the brain or was it 2%. Einstein used more than 4%. He ran his left hand through his wet hair. The sweet testosterone pituitary dribbled grease in his fingers. He used the drip on his dick. There was a Zen hum. The syncopated chirp of a bird on a limb he chose as rhythm to a menagerie, a chunk of gray the size of a grizzle stuck on a floss in the teeth was a blockage to the seismic mal-abnormalities recta dizziness, a shift to a needle rubs at a vinyl disc pricks to the pull. The kitchen with flies was inviting to a cook to cook, the slightest shake only scares the smallest insects. He drank of a hallowed juice jar water with rinds of limes, house plants watered less often than he. Diane knocked on the door. "Hello, open up!" she said, "Social Services." He could hear laying in bed. She woke him.

Diane peeked closely to the peephole and then the keyhole, shook the knob on the handle. "Open up!" she knocked on the door. There was no answer.

Step 3

The fever Boris had was uncanny. He saw spots. The rushed feeling of things he had to do stalled in his throat like an arsenic varnish on the roof of his mouth, he swallowed with his deft figure laying on his side underneath a double layer of wool blankets. The sweat on his forehead, on his arched eyebrows on the sunlight coming from above. There was a freedom of obligations. He was an Aquarius. His horoscope was yesterday's *rain is tonight's snow but only in your sleep, so take care to not take on any lodgers.*

The faculty assumed he was a problem on account where he lived, and because he was a half of something, which demands he round the half up to a whole. He told no one. There were meetings at the Principal's, he wanted to be placed higher, which he could not do, not even for a gifted boy whose arithmetic had an exponent. He had studied intensely for his test of citizenship. He was afraid to opt out of the name stuck like a sticker on a banana bunch washed in the sink (the peel inedible loses nothing by the glue). Of the naturalization of citizenry he asked, "I'll send you a book of my ancestry, but just one. For my mother you'll have to make a list I sold to a deranged boy rolled along with his clenched cheeks as a cat would strut proud of a bird the ants like... a lilac."

"Commies R' Us," a girl name Laura said to him as he sat before class, "we don't want you here. There're no seats," she was in favor of copy cat antics. The doubles won. They were better. Chairs scratched against the ceiling by the classroom above their heads as the class dismissed, "only when realized," he was ignoring her somewhat, "you entertainer," he said but found the machine a difficult bunch to bargain.... for her beauty resembled the ballerina that pops out of the jewelry tin. The tune was Tchaikovsky's *Swan Lake* and the gears provided an organist the chair which skated like a goose. If he hadn't seized at that exact time if he had an infatuation felt before his heart would have burst. She was immaculate. She was the type to get through her thesis work, had the credentials but was the wrong fit. She had the motivation posters with the company logo. The woman who had her job was a firecracker who earned the prestige they had. Her aging caught the school by her sudden retirement. It was doubtful the school which was run like a company had endured nearly three decades would last through the new year. The reputation floated on faculty suddenly dismissed or quit on her. If killing with kindness was given more often than the students may have understood why Boris after getting through the gruesome three weeks had been told he was no longer on the project, to work alone, or to be independent. He transported his bass on one wheel, had a hat for each day of the week. He met Laura. She told him she met her husband on Craig's list classifieds. He didn't ask. He was strung along like a kitten to a line of a kite, and her choice was that he finally be let go, or cut free. There was this and that. For celebrating the high holidays he was a whitefish thrown in the ice box for freezing until a later date. By the by, Boris was a dreamer and was eerily mistook for a dogs' scraps, but in his mind the vibrant shades the city drew color to him. He knew she was by the by her stare over the table drawing lines on her wrists. They talked for hours, her topic was weddings and before he could see anything she told him her mother was a dream interpreter and she knew he was hooked. She tossed like a trout at the pond sups. He was told no longer be with her, and later restricted although he had to eschew.

"No, I don't," Liz said after school to him tapping his opened fingers on the basses shoulder. Did he lift? He didn't have to. Dolly had a sewing machine, an old model which cost her seventy-five dollars. "Does your mother sew?" he had asked her. "If you've ever seen a seamstress press her thumb and pull the cloth, the hand pressed between the needle," and she knew he was tense. He did not want to talk with her dryly, which she was. He had a pencil. She didn't have one. She had lost what it was she was going to say. He had to roll his contrabass on one wheel home with wide hips and thin shoulders.

The paths diverged once more. A fresh intake care to lend your trust to strangers, you'll get new returns on the things you gave, the fortune in the paper contradicted her fortune cookies', *only beauty is skin deep, there is a forest of words beneath a twig of vice. Beware those things mine depth in mundane after all, a tiny snap of the spheres means big news.* Rain had been forecast, and the girls hurried to the car which drove to Lonnie's. "I don't wanna kill my china pig," Zoë recited Captain Beefheart's lyrics. Her Leo horoscope was *notes as you go about your day the equinox, and the blowing sky.* "I'm a classical guy, and you have an ear for songs," he strummed a few jangling strings on a guitar listening for overtones of a note, the type heard when piano keys cling on a tuneless thing. "If the shoe fits," he told her. "You hear the song ever?"

"You didn't hear the recitative," Margery said with her china doll eyes carved in ivory. A painter gave her sharp figures a burnt hue. The house was a shack in the woods with a pretty Asian girl reciting as the song said, "One little girl used t' put her fingers in his snout. I put uh fork in his back," by a naive Sagittarius at the foot of the stage enchanted by them let out a, "No I don't."

"Well I used t' go t' school with uh' little red box 'n I used to have m' pig go with me we walked for blocks," and as she understood him made a decision to turn the lives over to the cue of God. One courteous seeks the changes. He could lick the shit off of her ass. He saw the prison. He was in it. He became a cliché at last by disobeying curfew violating parole. The lake in an upscale neighbors' yard was vandalized with a sewage pipe overflowing. The capers' blame fell on the city for a pipe broke, which was old and overused. He detested the knowledge of others, and his plots were as silent as a doll behind a glass plane. He talked to the things he sees, and drew fans to the paltry whose lives were the golden apples wise Athena threw as promises to her suitors.

"I fed the neighborhood it was uh big neighborhood," Lon said. He had outlined in his notebook exactly the next steps. He'd convince the girls to take part, and knew who'd be the hardest, and whom to convince initially. He had a short past with one of the girls. An Opera showiness like a psychologist with dry boogies, or a grease monkey contemplating a machine's emptiness. Lon's meetings with people fitted his soul with sexual gratification. She wore drying mascara on blue contact eyes and told the end of some joke. Lon met her by a classified ad. "Some jobs are bad. They hurt. I'd want you to know why. Why anyone can be good, good only," Deidra argued with her lip in her teeth. She bit her lip. It bled. He had to flee the room before talking about health concerns he had had once. No shade in the parking lot where Lon quite randomly ran in her while at the bank machine.

He asked in a staccato for a one night stand. Her vocal scrapings in a golden lens of horn rimmed glasses as if to say I know, yes I know.

A fem Policewoman in the bicycles visor with the gold trim and a whitish hue an egg chickens lay bleached, white stamped with a pink receipt. Had his hand on his jaw slobbering. Had to wipe his corner of his lip on his shirt. Had on short sleeves buttoned with a left pocket stuffed with lottery tickets. Deidra and he went to the horse races. Running in the mud sank *Mind That Bird* behind *Rachel* 'round the track a line of stallions, which is the true horse power of a car in Lon's garage. Beer cans infield dropped which was illegal to bring from outfield. Outlaws the booze prohibited for horses. "Say it'll kill yah," Lon said in an implosion of grief tore tickets into confetti.

At a Marriot hotel he agreed to fuck after a long friendship was sunk. It was a naval disaster only when all her clothes were on the floor did she be with him. He came so close. Their lips inhaling. Her sweat touched his upper lip, the voluptuous pink puckered on decidedly amber. She'd try to stay unattached to things, and to her the things most dangerous were spooning on the sofa with the wool sheets pulled over. The crude jokes she told while laying in bed on her belly farting. Or the way he swung his leg over her.

"I've had one felt under the knife," he said in quotes, "and you didn't want me to feel pain. I didn't feel any. But you thought I was," he said wanting to hold onto her. "I thought you would yell," he wanted to say. She was terrified at his ache. He wanted her to stay the way she was. His sack was plump and big. "Don't get up," she said and dressed in her blouse and dress. "I am sick," he said, "you can see." He held his sides. He was completely nude by the door ready to leave in the nude with the covers. He made no move to shelter or chase. He really wanted to know her. "Art was right about you. You are strange," Deidra said last she saw Lon. Here he was trying to convince her.

"Costuming is very popular in the porn scena," Lon said finally. He was trying to make a scene. Arthur was filming. "Natal," Liz cried out to her, Margery, who in wet paint on the sand wood drawing a circle and right triangles in a thick brush in globs of white oil which never wash with water. She wanted no part. The theme was: the three daughters of the General had guests over a plate with toast points and pieces of cheese. The Swiss triangles were acute, an oblique a gal in a Coors hat rolled a horn out of the wax paper lining the dish and blew out a natal note. Lon was a visiting aristocrat humorously had a tuning fork in his conch shell of an ear. The camera filmed the tulip trees' lavender blossoms drooped by the second floor victor brand aluminum window. The two girls were the youngest daughter and the countess. Zoë squeaked in pink rubber boots while she came in from being locked out, the recording picked up a low frequency, a key fiddling the hall which was dark in the rainy weather masking the natural day. The brass lamps stood by the tan sofa was artificial spotlight bright yellow on the star in a black polyester skirt thigh-high, her push bra of an Italian clothier beneath the nipple the wire ran fit for a size smaller than hers which was swapped in a used bin marked on sale with a price tag framed askew with the digital recorder. She was the older one in clothes much too tight. Her pastel blouse clashed with ink jet dyed slick hair with the hose stopper right on the ankle, and the raincoat draped over her orange sherbet. The middle child Liz had cum soaked hair which stuck beneath Lon's fingers. He shook before the mirror before the shoot. The rubber rain dew films her eyes round as a flying saucers' only seen in flashes, which never seemed to blink, even once. Only once the damp saturated the blouse of pastels. Her slick jet hair had pearl ribbon, a sheer veneer with the shimmy of the rain drops. Lonnie stroked fondly at her hair on her cheeks until there were red blisters on her skin where the makeup smears.

Arthur put the camera on a stand, and the careful eye of the General entered the flat view of the movie screen. Art wore a grey suit with impromptu hair, and this was his only filming. His short role was to coerce

Margery. She eventually gave in, or was worn down by the seemingly endless live streaming. There was a machine with a dildo on a sliding metal pole in the closet which was carried on the set. He framed the camera on her face, which Boris always told her was a pretty one, and her hair which was long then spilling all over the rug in amber waves and chest as the apparatus was on the floor beside the foot of the table, the video spanned out: sister was on the aristocrat on the tan sofa and Margery was occupied by an apparatus.

"You have to have a sense of humor about these things," Lon told her, and her friends after the scene had airtime on the you porn internet domain.

"I only wanted to help out," Margery said. She was livid over seeing herself with the pads of the pistons pressed between her legs. The paint cans on the floor carpet of the car which drove to the garage had stayed there, the lids stained with purples, and pinks like a circus geek takes a drink of toxicants. He took no care to cover the paraphernalia. Boris would never care. Arty starved during the day, only supping for mother so the teachers' assistant noticed he was behaving oddly because he was hungry. The teachers' assistant took his groaning personally and sent him to the Principals. The rest never noticed his hunger, but found his humor to be unfunny. He was worse off for her sight. A maintenance made the joke Arty and Boris were like infants tossed in the air and shot at by the Sheriff. He

51

said, if either of their mothers made a claim for one to let live. Arty had a maid Olga. She'd sometimes make a claim for him, yet had several domiciles to clean and dry cleaning to retrieve.

Like fumbling in the dark for the sticky sap to put on the horsehairs for the bow to strike coarser on the strings when he was moved to get up. Dolly was the last to go while Boris' dad was doing the taxes and had to be on his way before long. He was in the business of bootlegging new movie releases on the big screen. The early shows booked last. A horsefly always biting at the heels of everyone at home and in the neighborhood was a legend, was an anonymous face in the dark theater lit only by dusky aisle lights which hardly led anyone to find their light. He was fed the camera like an usher's flashlight cut through darkness. Boris' nights were laying awake in bed contemplating sitting in the grass with action figures, the arms pulled off. He had an armless wrestler with one-leg clenched tightly in his fist. The metal parts were cold, and the cold gave nightmares. The hollow figures were out of focus all in a row running the bed span along iron beams. He had a fever, and sleep came suddenly in the hot air fogged street under the glass.

He took a passenger in the dawns' crack who stated plainly, "need a ride, I uh."

Boris pressed the automatic window switch a space small enough to let a fly crawl through which made a conveyer belt sound as the vacuous passenger with unappealing odor crept in beside Boris, the stereo knob set to none. The stranger exposed the tiniest groove along a diminishing figure an abdominal scar which appeared to make him smaller than before. He insisted he needed a twenty. Boris gave him it. With his mundane encounters the strangers he met were alien. He had to relive uncounted meetings with the simplest irreverence or the comparison with a psychosis which the frame unsettles slightly rendering the things beyond his sight first invisible, secondly tyrannical. The longing grew almost impossible to deal with. That which stored in his room were overflowed with dampness. The plug under the door let. Unheard stolid shapes were locked out, would listen yet be unable to cope. With him always, he was followed by the droning of tires. He was tossed to the sound. His ears stopped with earwax. He told Boris, he was a nurse, that he had once lived in Annapolis before his divorce, and went to Baltimore where he'd grown older in Huntington. The houses bent over like old men on the faded wood stoops, the painted splinters of slums. He had amassed debt which had to be lent, and a charge at the bank was impending or else. He'd never see the rent and the heat was off for everyone which didn't seem fair, and to be sure, he waved with his hand where. "Over there, that's where I live."

Boris felt thick as the sea. He was fueled by good influences on the places where he drove. Right now he didn't feel so hot. He didn't want his trust wrecked by dishonest things. He was set back most by doubletalk which was inconsistent like the stranger said later: 'He was a house painter', which seemed reasonable. He was a nurse, and a house painter. He was cracked, and his name was something everyone called him Mike 'N Ike.

His phone was missing an area code, yet it was the details that were absent which were easiest to forgive. He was affronted by an awesome aromatic mint mouthwash of the gin tinged cologne. He was red in the face.

Someone he never met before. He had no distrust of. He took the twenty whose celebrity is on the face of neither guessed at. He was telling a sea shanty. He gave a dollar for gasoline. The passenger jibed at by perfuse shame. He was bloodletting money. That was holding on to keeping him down. He was feeling better, much better that he gave. A dollar's too small for the time, and the nickel is the new five dollar, and the dime is a twenty. He thought how much of a schmuck he made him feel by believing the yarn and getting tangled with it. His paw in the thread only pulled him in deeper. Twenties were like bloodletting leeches clung to his legs sucking at the fat. The letting sucked red marks on his heels, which peeled off slippery in the lint traps of a pocket. He had went in the river with his pants' cuff upturned and the water rushing at his ankles pull at the loose pores. A stain of crimson on iridescent fluctuations. He knew how to overdraw however much he had in the bank. "Drive to the old swimming hole," Boris thought to himself. He did not hear the name Mike gave because the car was too fast, and the garbled sound rushed like the ocean warbles in the concave seashells.

He was at the kitchen table addressing a letter, 'Dear Greta.' An envelope unfilled by a nut filled in a chocolate on the unsealed plastic used to wrap the box. It was open. He left it out that morning before penning the letter. He had stamped the envelope Express with too much postage due. He wanted to tell her all those things. He was dumb. He went for a drive. He was driving with Mike. They drove by a pale yellow patch of grass on a stale slope. There was a pit bull pulled by a rope tied to a brown shoe. He tore through the leather, and snapped at the boyish hands teasing the monster with the blind hunger. He stiffened in the leg. The gas line shot through the pipe to the engine, and the stranger went along for the ride with him at a steady speed. The red line on the RPM monitor flung, it leapt. He sawed the wheels fast through his foot on the car carpet crick a grayish-white asphalt like a meat hammer on ground chuck which has dried the fresh, red cut a gray, bled dry and a congealed fat. "You can let me off here," Mike said, and got out the car. He went to make a phone call at a payphone.

Boris drove off to steer in a bell curve to the stoop where he left that morning, and he never got Mike's name, or his area code.

"Hello, hello, hello, Mike," Rudy said with the receiver in hand, "I raped you," he said to Mike. The AA group had had an ongoing discussion on inconstancy with the partners affected by alcoholics.

"You should not joke about those cum-heads," Mike said to his sponsor. Fucking cum-heads were his real thoughts. The list of those killed by his automobile grew by one more last year. He wanted to put an end to the circle of pregnancy and births. The hooligans seemed to him a threat. "Blame the organizer, or the sponsor," Mike said, "blame yourselves." On the phone, noon, whines: maid quitting interfering with being at the meetings. The group met Monday-he's never in attendance but as his buddy liked to say was tended to. Before the maid quit she cited the habits which were most upsetting to her. The worst was he became distracted constantly. He looked up always. She was sweeping, and the brush needles harassed Rudy to nervous shaking fits. The depth of Rudy's conscience sunk in when he was quietest. It was with deep regret he became aware his mother's absence. A drink emptied the glass. He counted her flaws. He held up three against her. He was four. The cycles of the many rhythms of her laughter preceded her first daughter having her first son at a younger age than she. He patiently wanted for her to misstep, and when she did, he did. She held him to a crooked line and he was hers to do with she pleases. Mike often attended the meetings with a gun in his cool pants.

Diane was paralyzed usually in the morning, but Chris had been lazing with her legs greased fondling her lover and herself awake. She kissed the earlobes, stroked her temples. The heart made hard penetrated her. She began to shake. So did she. The warm morphine flow needled below her abdomen curbed her appetite, and she pushed harder the way her drive gave way. Christine gave. She gave and fell over. "I'm a rape," Christine told her, agape.

"No, you," Diane said, "You're a grape."

"You did," she said. "That wasn't me, it was you," she said, "that wanted." The pain Diane had was worse. She knew whom she spoke of. There was an irony in her work fastened on her sleeve white cuffs. An affair destined for nowhere, which was every other second in the day, and on an off day a slum row with nothing except the gutted wiring, pink insulation silver lining and exposed wood was her home. She committed herself to a prison sentence. She began to shape a replacement for her vices, so the sting would hurt less. She saw her come into work at the cubicle beside hers. The cork vapor furtively drifts through a particle board.

Her someone else drank for her. Diane was happy like the pinch of a splinter removed that prick and the pinches grew fatter between her index and ring.

Step 4

The Po shot a radio signal at the driver; in the seat the one cents in the jar shook; the car frame jostled slightly; the thin protective plastic hybrid whose shattered glass drove him. His mind flipped by the tintinablation in his mind, he said, "Never pay no mind," he stepped onto the boulevard to tell the awkward old man whose rolled down drivers' side hung his white spotted head out the door. Drumming his fingers on the dash before the rear end collided drove around Rudy red in the face of Boris Borisovich's auto. In the east the pedestrian barely eleven like water sits standing in a puddle, the mosquito's mother lays her larvae. He lays hit in the street runs forever in a pose jumping a hoop. The plumbing never moves like an old houses' sinks cough dust as if the trap with wax clogs and the honking cars having nothing to do as if he is one more stop, just a lie sleeping on the road, the rider squeezes by. The weathers' moist spoils attracted a gang of slugs hid beneath brown and yellow leaf sheets on the drive she drove over backing out in the morning. By the end of the day the dusky odor perforated her. She never went out.

The clear liquid the consistency of cerebral spinal fluid by the postman hunched over with a blue raincoat had retrieved nothing sent by her either. The post rang the house next door to hers with something she signed for start her in a napping chair. She was an ugly girl. She was ugly as a monstrosity. Chris told her so, even separated she had made regular visits to her doorstep. She drove by the street her house was on every day. Diana was kind, sensitive and wanted her close-by. Christine just herself was a tightly closed hand with the strength of ten men, she beat into Diane. The insult stung. Herself immaculate. "You're homely," she told her gal. "Always keep the latch lock parallel," Chris motioned to the welcome mat, "when you go out. Shut it."

"You won't let me in," and Diane was a diamond in the rough compulsively obedient, yet wounds her pores. The jargon of fat cats at the typewriters poised by the office windows were attracted to a house of glass, the wind tore her palms against and the rain poured her sorrows through a sieve which pounded the glass, was a frog preserved in formaldehyde, an embryo in water smudged fingers press against run with the news, a fog when the clouds were dry and a print draped the houses' light.

Boris Borisovich knew he was worthless. He had a toenail infection a sliver grew greener, and a worse ulcer which was the fault of an infected gallbladder.

After the thing in him was surgically removed, was in a jar so he could see, the herring caught in him extracted and resold to pay the doctors and surgeons. He was crushed. The car dent had scraped paint on the owner's automobile. In an altercation he was prepped to contact a lawyer, or a suit was the reaction. The things he did affected him deeply. He wore his heart on his sleeve. He went to the woods to shoot at seabirds in a flock by the airport in a cluster of branches with a bruised diesel on the edge. Sometimes the loud motor of a plane shook the forest where he was.

"Are those seabirds bothering you," James asked Boris' son, "or are they migrated yet?"

"'tis the stream," Boris laughed about the roommates now they had moved on. He was no longer boarding at the house, he had floated to. His father sent him there. James was surreptitious with queer things, and illegal migrants. He was employed at the cannery, retired. The plant bottomed up, and had plucked for his hobbies, yet had little to do with those he'd worked with. James was younger than. His retirement was labor sympathetic for the causes he searched forth. They saw the clippings in the news, the symphonies' lauded and he read the type on sight, and so did he.

"Those you knew seem to forget you," Deb said, "you assume they've died," her phrase was a line curved in a nose which suddenly drooped into a lip, "or they, you're dead."

The sides of the hall thick with laughter up the braced columns like trembling teeth and the musicians filed in the same peculiar fashion that notes were syllables which once found were the tones they represented, the things they did. The night was a second awakening a python smoked the sunrise high in the thick black the sunsets took too, too long.

"We'll see about that re-hair," James said, "like when faggots pull out my hair," he said bending low displaying male pattern baldness the sparrows pecked at. "Well, you see. I don't know your father, Boris. We've never met, that's why."

The fuse unstrung, a white horse hair plucked on one direction where the hand held the bow by friction was clipped with a sharp thumbnail in a curved serpentine embrace with the flat finger pad print on the point of the rose hued stick. The bow dropped to him hung shivering with the milliseconds. There was a grenadier. He saw the textures of the sounds of the quay birds and he rushed in the fray. The fire only she saw, he went to quell a cold shiver his coal shaped eyes' steam. *Belay for her.* Her dipped on the violin a squeal like a pig. Her chin dipped in the rest which drew short staccato beads of sweat her hair drawn in a bow slanted into her violin whose atonal colors sprang from her heart, the low dive in her bosoms silk bathed in a slender train, bangs a note, the craving the wreck of the caboose whose rounds spun like pinwheels. The train boards' lit up with the waves anguish as the particles blew up estimated arrivals, and she stood exactly there, there where the bomb tore the steel engine just outside of a minor stop on the way to a five of three. The desires for her world an empty room was sadly broken by the commotion, went outside to see the noise, which bled the stripe. His soul flew. The urge to tell her he never had had. The rush in his arteries collapsed in the veins, constantly looking that a sparrow flew might land at his corroded tip for bread pieces he had none of. He spotted the sparrow.

The houses in the west side were thin and tall figures leaning against a shared stonemasonry. There was a false feeling of smallness. A huge living room hardwood floors gave under short footsteps in deep basements. The large Victorian windows hall to high ceiling shook him from the insides. Boris was rehearsing the Bach Suites. The instrument was worth a fortune hiding behind form stone, wood and the blade in the shirt pocket knife he used to cut loose horse hairs from the bow was his charm against the creaking floor boards whose every step petrified the hairs on his arm. An intruder outside of the cellar curled in the crawl spot between the kitchen pantry was in a damp deposit of moisture hanging below the stone frame on the steps leading below the base. The murk in the puddle he hid in grew dirty, damp grass. The slugs, the maggots use for shelter like rubber. The pencil marked the Suite.

The mud on hands on the stone was thinner. Boris moved closer to find the tone. He had his ear to the F-holes. Kaleidoscope color burned from the bowels of the contrabass.

The intruder crept behind him. He had a gun to his ear, the one towards the instrument. Boris' hand had the bow in his one hand, and the razor to cut the loose hair, and one hand was empty. He knew he might have a last chance to live, his life or the bass whose value he knew was only a few empty hits. He shoved the knife beneath his armpit, and the gunshot went off below his ear deafening him. The bullet either took off his ear and the thing he wrestled for was the music he loved, or the head he might lose.

He bled a red line to the front door, and Boris was bleeding too. He dialed on the phone, but misdialed. The operator said, "If you like to make a call please hang up and try again." He no longer heard the tone. Boris lost the connection to hear, atonally. A lass leaning a text between her aped cleavage across the street caved just under her slender shoulders the arch of the Victorian window than the frame where she weighing above the waist sat her head against bathed in red on the brick row.

Lon drove across town. There was a holdup in the gas station window where the wagon landed. He filled up the tank with regular. The digits on the counter directed him to see the cashier. She was held up with a tiny pistol in a wide sleeve. He had a jacket with many pockets. The cashier was in terror.

"I'd like a receipt," Lon said. Her fat arm on a barrel bust handed him a long one. He saw the blood in her eyes cry and roar. She rolled her whites. He took the paper and in his hand made a gang sign. The holdup kept her talking, and his accomplice said, "let's get out." Lon had the paper fisted in a hammer; the sign of the Soviets.

In three inches of a softly streaming brook Lon had his cheek on a rock, a chipped tooth and tried to breath in through his nose. Lon was swallowing some water. The shirt muddied like gunshot sails. He had a little headache. He was at the end of his, but his partner had a tougher *bon voyage* than he. Boris was locked-in a copper wire birdcage, put on his nerves the fear of dying. He never cried ever since. He just shut up, shut out. The ear to the water tuned in, tuned out.

A long painted train, russet as a leaf in the station wind. The bell rang; the ground froze by the tracks where the crossed the river stones rusted corrugated iron beside the new iron; the sound was chased until the very last bell where Lon last saw standing there. Boy he had him on his mind, yet in the colorless drapes in the night the victims of the dead reared their ugliness the mirrored shield Perseus held at the head of the stairs whose long serpent tongue snapped at the foot. Here in a drawer were the receipts in case the taxes filed wrong were audited by the secret bureau. At night Boris Borisovich shot a hunting rifle in a grass field as a swift warning to something out there in the night. The crackling gunplay resolve was the type of rake neighbors admired. In irate thirst a bullet fly in a dull thud to take away the living thing.

Dolly's hole in a stockings' tactile smooth sheer on the vine leafy thorns stuck too sharply to the deep bricks sunk in the dirt crease along the fingers' width crust of the wall which shook at every attempt to pull him up. The whole of hers in the hole of his. Her legs slipped through the silk. A runner down the street by a corner went around her toe dove like a heron, the sepia reeds in the seeping gray bleach drained from the reds, the thought of her on the dive.

"I am African" Pierre's daughter said. By her exposed toes the albino in the west side trees the yellow leaf by leaf the dandelions bulbs. To those who have never caught a pigeon bare handed in the feather. He got the heron.

In the sandbox the whole block had the odor of the stray cats' litter. Tunnel sight of a barrel with no depth, a cloudy milk in the crying tears which set the stray in a circle. He could see the sparrow swiped away. All hours spent after the sun rose with the carcasses of three chickens boiled in a pot of steaming water. Steam stuck in the olfactory. "Can you smell me little bird?" said tattered in a pot of chicken stock bathing in the vapors until the skin on every pore soaks with the bird sweat. Opens the glands with most secretions in the armpits, the anus. The mouth open wide shows teeth if caught on the scent, the small fry should fly right in the cook's esophagus, a trick learned from Saint Frank that'll suck the grease off the sparrows' wing.

"The cat had a cataract," the tattered man wrote his pith observations. "I am sculptor of the line fragments. Times are choicest for ever who is fit to be, and not to be," the dogmatic verse dogged of the poor angelic verse. "Whose mercy we forgive, the pain pity vice," the tape player reeled the strip, "the easy chose to cull the corruptors of man. I am murderer, man," repeats the recording said, "man murders." The typeface said instruct how to a roulette wheel fires a pistol in a set of chairs randomly at sin is to the sinner, the ball and jacks or a rubber ball to the cup with string attached, the games small boys have, or toys youths never forget.

Basking in the reeds by the river beside the narrow street in the trees netted a bell over the steep hop with his feet in the air and slid nearly shoeless with the sewn tare into the pale grass. The grass was pale closer to the city lockup. Here was greener. The blanch reeds yellowing by the sun drenched. The mud bore the heel. He sunk toe-deep. Lon was nervous no one might ask him for a loan, a loan never repaid, than he was tricked, or in a ruse. He bottomed with generousness. Even grazed by a truck, yet never refused a ride. There's a smoke crowded dive of a place. Easy drinkers generally soak ice with hard gin moving in the darkness, darkness moves. He can find himself only in an off centeredness pull him along a divergent path where some like to stare at the trash by a building which has been there so long.

On the second floor a Dutch immigrant gives free hash stogies for nothing and all night indulgers come and go, yet two seem to stay around chiding those in the tendency to give them a ride where they live far in the west side. The nettling becomes hard to decipher. "I told him," Kay says, "right after I finish my cigarette."

"You want a ride?" Lonnie asks, "I'm going that way, and have nothing else to do." The pounding of heavy metal on the floors pushes the two shivering at the knees to exit through the downstairs. Lon's already in the car. Joe says, "we got to," and listens to the rock, "bartenders' she'll give a ride."

When two strikes she says get out, no way she's driving out that way and "you can't sleep here." There's a bed in the back for the owner of the dive hole. He pays the land rent. Lon gave the thought. He lets the car warm up for a few minutes.

Lon see's in the obits a 17 and 18 year boys found in separate parts of east Baltimore supposedly connected in origin. They disperse the same location and where the mouth feeds neither guessed at. The turn breaks to split ends, the dirt scrapes beneath the fingernails. Cops take evidence: wrist studs, tin clip piercing, leather and details collect in Lon's mind of a trapped hares' splitting at the rifle sounds.

After the night was dead walkin' in the stranger parts of the east Joe says he's going nowhere. "Fine," Kay says. He walks in a street bathed in silence, whereas Joe steps up to a gang standing streetwise. He says he wants a cut of the purple vine. Money, hand it over. He shows a miniature revolver rifling in Joe's pockets turns running shot bleeds on the street. Kay's walkin' at a faster pace than he was. He hears the bang what could be a bullet. He's at the train stop trying to put a spot where the spark went out, see's someone stand beside the tracks. Wave for him to come on over. Herds him three streets away to a dip in the ground which splatters a waxy drip. Lon can stay in no longer, takes a drive to the gunpowder river. The car careens off the road, gets on the dirt to cross over, the heat of the furnace reeks of carbon fumes. He's still unsure it's they've who've listed in the obits.

He took pleasure. The wiretap was for him only, yet because of his act all were condemned to share his sin. She was sweet sixteen only, and her debut caused a stir at the other end of the phone line, where everything was recorded on a white metal disc. The reel was revolving.

Step 5

"This is my last cig," Boris said, and they left him to ruminate the rest of the night on his cig. The other end of the line Lon told him a rash of gas station robberies triggered a hike in gas prices where the property tax was lower than letting a bunch of balloons go at once like a bundle of spaghetti strangled, snuffed the string, dents limp limberly. "We are the targets of it," Lon plum said newly laid off. "He said he'd kill me. I told him to. We'd chase mice, and go ice skating."

"Art," Boris said.

"I got the gold medal, though Arty was the better ice skater. He had the copper, and let out a yell as I ran passed him. He saw me jump up on the blades off my skates which was unfair. That's just the way things are. I didn't even want to win, but I took it."

"He showed me the hurt, I saw him. He hardly knew me," Boris said, "just passers-by on the stairs to some victor. That morning he was getting dressed with his shirt buttoned the wrong side top bottom, not bottom top. His shoelaces untied, and his sleeves undone. He didn't bother," he said, "when Margery took him by the hand to grab the socks he clutched tightly to the thing, and he was a thing of adoration

70

after. The actor wore rouge which made his mother blush, and everyone needed to know how he was. I knew," he said, "I did because there is a brief snapping before the conductor strikes the orchestra to rush in like a match on a stone. He didn't move and knew just where to put himself under the tree, the one with the white branches, and when too. I wrote a poem about that tree where the librarian found him hung, and I saw the suffer his eyes showed me, and I told him where to die."

"He died by car crash," Lon said, "stonewalled the Jackson where his father bought the old car. He was a highway runner, and the burn was in his arteries, his blood."

"No, not him. You didn't know him. I knew him."

"Yes, he talked in a frank tone," Lon said, "some consider righteous, but not me."

"I got my best thoughts in the car where my thoughts came to me at no particular hour in the day," Boris said, "he wanted to touch others. He had a good soul, an old one."

"Didn't he have that weird teacher," Lon said, "the one who was let go."

"She was of a school of thought demanded she reach out to grab him by the larynx to shape the note through by restricting his airflow. He let her though he took no pleasure."

"She had a cold stare," Lon said.

"She was on fire with a short charge to grasp his neck like electricity. It was his neck to strangle, him!" Boris said, "it singes the hairs in my throat. Pushing the sand through the organ."

"The boy wanted to get his hands on anything," Lon said, "it was urged by someone closer, a soda he leaned into the straw sip with his nose."

"He was dragged to the floor by her fingers thick as octopus tendrils. His face blanched blue."

"I took a girl to the mountains," Lon said, "it was a big off-road vehicle. She wanted to drive. I let her. And she took the wheel and drove the thing off the road onto these huge rocks. We bumped in the air and when we hit the tire blew. I had to get out an' change it. All we could see was mountain to mountain in the hills. I'd gather sticks to set in a pyramid, rolled up newspaper on the floor mats I'd use to start the flame. If I had some matches. Not my best," Lon said. "This was a girl, who'd want to ask her 'want to pick up sticks' in a rustic country house, but in the mountains with quite a few clouds. I took a branch and swung back till my back was sore in the shoulders and everything blew. She sat in the car, pretty, I saw her in the mirror's turn-"

"There is no love, the romance of the world is gone," Boris said.

"Out the window kept an eye on the tire pressure, the repairs were underwent and paid for," Lon said. "I just wanted to crawl in a ditch and weep. The UV were sunrays everywhere in the light and darker places. I hid in a damp basement with the dust on the cooling air-filtration system. The blowing yellow tape in the vent like a flapping flag, silent sounds of water running an underground river out of a pocket of a lake. Drove me insane with longing. The sticks gave me cuts, too."

To the quiet dialogue of his, he said nothing. "I heard the voice," Lon said, "and it smarts." There was smirking. "I stuck my finger in an electric socket to feel white waves. Had to do something for the pain."

"I saw a neurologist about this unidentified object in my brain. It stung like a leech. The nurse said to me that all brains are unique, yours is just different," Boris swung his head with the phone in hand to his ear. "Let's get married I told Margery. Let's have four boys and a girl, one for each street that intersects here. Let's name after the street signs," Boris said, "I told her the first kiss. She called me up."

"There are only four street intersections," Lon said.

"No, there are only two. Boris Borisovich, that's a name," Boris told Lon, "the son of Boris."

"She always was the sad song." Lon was laughing at the other end. In the silence of voices he heard his mother calling the sound came through the line.

"A girl asked me for a pencil, or a pen. I had one. She wore a pretty yellow dress and was round, her groove apple red." He had lubricant for his used records on a desk drawer. "It's poison to the touch."

Here was the old recording the eavesdropper had. He had earplugs as simultaneously new dialogues were ripped on the magnetic strip. "Her love flower, I have no better word. I'd my arm around a bass clef sign," Boris said, "the crook laying on her side. The mattress sank under the wood bar where I keep my rock candy. A curly slash white blink an eye I saw inky shadows clasp on her a treble sign. We shook the florist's roses. Seed petals germinate fluttering in the soft glow. The television was blaring a blue light. Her dark lines became an old man with a pipe."

"He's your old man, and she's his wife," Lon said interpreting the dream.

"My old man was a plumber," Boris said shifting seamlessly from dreams to life.

"The women really get to me. I never went to pick up honeys at bars. I went to the types of places homos are. All those signs to signal a girl you're into her, only her and no one else, or no. I never was taught by anyone. I've the body language yes and no gays have. There's a pinch-it's a thumb knuckle!"

"It's hard to crack that walnut. Try crushing a grape with your big toe," Boris joked.

"No, I've enough to get through a sentence at a 'country' minimum security prison."

"I can," Boris said conclusively, "act tougher than you are. The girls lived through me. I was too soft dust to dust out of there to get a Scotch Bourbon somewhere else. No school can hold me. Too cool."

"That's an old fashioned thing. You're too fast for her," Lon said. "You should've had the tape. It starred your Margery. We've plans in the new production of a film. I've listed an ad on a porn topic thread for German groups of either sex, and Russians too!"

"You!" Boris exclaimed and slammed the phone head on a pile of books.

"I'll show you the one we have up for the world to see a gang of hooligans featuring your bitch," Lon said jokingly.

Boris hung up the phone in the ear. He was in his dark thoughts when he saw the narrow streets. It was then he said the Lord's Prayer and saw it in himself, 'girl fucks something,' he pondered in the interrupted space between the beeps on the dial, 'meets a boy, same thing, only difference we did it with no computers.' The phone picked up.

"She called me on the phone. I argued about where to hook up. We argued the whole thing. Longer than a year seems only a month we're always shouting. It was over and we went to the hills to convince ourselves. We drown sorrows, red wine fly away all cares to care for to take care it's terrible. It's terrible. No time down. He's two beers lapses under weight, oh the starving soul, at the wake I drank a twelve broke the caps to laugh at sorrows an ear to a bottle; an echo to a seashell;

the short list, or those that made it to the people close to me are the spattered spot of keys. I was looking for the key and found a bottle. An ear put the modes to listen, the soft flow of the toilets' hum, I hear a voice calling. It is a near and dear, you."

"Don't hang up the phone," the suicide hotline operator shouted.

"At night we pretended to be the workers in the dog-eared morning. Jim drove a truck to the market on ice with the fish freshly netted and still stench in the crates. I drank to keep alert. The pitch of dark gets on my every last nerve. I told Jim all sorts of things I'd pretended to know a lot about. He began to take classes at the learning annex. Craziest thing I once asked if he'd ever done something really wrong he'd regret. The white light gets to me. I bought junk with my paycheck: used records, paperbacks and VHS, that type of older blues singers sang. I even dreamt once I told Bill Evans I was Lightning Hopkins."

"Stay on the line," the voice cried out.

"Put an ear to the dirt and the sound escapes. The dust shakes," Boris had his chafed ear on the carpet dirt, "it is the silent vibration swims to the rivers and lakes in the dusk. The hairs in the nostrils sweep the floors musky hurt. I can no longer take in the air. I see a blister sore cut with a sharp knife. The imprinted finger bleeds a deep crease below. Hello, is this suicide line?" Boris' dialing finger crunched the number pad-he lifted as the operator answered, yes. "I've been having suicidal thoughts. And I don't want to hear wisdom about dying, 'there's no railing on this ski boat,' 'the almighty looks on his flock'!"

"Over? Is the feeling still?" the woman's voice asked.

"I've took one step on the ledge to the street. I think I'll fly. I'm plucked. Never mind, someone once ran to the window. Arty had his violin out; he put the instrument in its case. Art listened to me sing an art song in tenor clef with the piano my good friend Jim keyed; through the wall he came in the door to the room, went near the already open window ledge. He took a few steps round like a pigeon. Jim and I said nothing."

The hotline operator had his mouth glued at the stitched seams.

"He's holding the soft pedal. I was about to snap but clicked my teeth when I talked," Boris said. "And I knew he was playing. I told him jump already, the jerk deserved no less."

"Did he?"

"No, he was trying to pull someone's string. Or, leg. Ye, the girl in the next room wouldn't have him edge her. We went a long way. He'd try tricks on a girl of thirteen he was two years older than and she let him have it. She didn't even want to, no, no one commits suicide with something heavy on heart."

"Let it out, let it out," the voice told him.

"He drank coffee. I saw the stain on his teeth. The fat bruised kidney bled puffy-like a fish-coffee is an anti-oxidant. He held his breath, a frightened hand knuckles pressed in the stomach to a scar deep in the belly a centimeter to a wound an old war wound a bayonet. The soldier in him seemed to rise up the face of limpid water. It was, he said in a detective voice, it was a knife. There was residue as a bullet shrapnel or fragments of debris. Sometimes he let his fingers free. The elliptical diaphragm rested on the bowels. There was no cancer. Someway the man lets me know he's okay. He's sick. He'd oxidize the pulse; the root of his wrist plucked from his sleeve."

"Still having those thoughts?"

"Still stuck on that boy," Boris said still as if Lonnie could hear, "ye, he could've fell under the wheel. I know if he knew the bicycle was on a collision to hit the truck; was he trying to play me chicken, to see if I'd step in the way; was the trucker in on it for some little ploy; was his intent to see if I'd the nerve to be brave, in his tribe the men are proud, strong. Was he testing me?" Boris wanted to know if he'd pass the test, too. "The thing has me tying my hair in knots. I was happier before the truck."

"It didn't," the voice said.

"No, it did not. Someone was murdered out of that house. A week later someone died on the nook beneath the marble stoop beside that house. A year has flown since in the alley beside the square a civilian gunned down. The night wails with gunshots in the air rang aloud on the grass strip. A mother cries for a lost son. The sun rises in the morning just the same," he set the receiver on the phone a half-click-

"No, don't hang up! The dream you were having!" the woman's voice shouted in the line.

"I suffocate my dreams. The sunup drooled on the pillowcase I dreamt in a lake the lights lit afire a maze of starry lamps. The horseflies bit. A telephone booth closed in the heart of a beast. An infected needle in the coin slot. I could feel the pulse. Crossing a cable bridge on a canal in a shady serene town. I walked into a scene with a fire swallowing gypsy caught in still life. She tossed torches stemmed from her hands juggled with pinpoints on a wheel between her legs a bright prism of sound, spinning."

The operator answered, "and?"

"Sightless staring the girl whispered in my ear. The pimp asked her if she forgot payment. Twenty euros. Airport cash counter aisle a client was flirting, she refused. Someone in her business shoe hi pumps had a bottle to share, they split-and in the bathroom dropped his pants. She felt obliged to oblige him. I'll never comprehend how she did that. The bang after me was a sales clerk at Macy's department. She told him she could not be with a one and only, and went to me too."

"Tell me about her," the voice said, relieved he was talking more sensibly.

"Art said to me, 'like,' the choir master said if he used the word 'like' he'd have to pay a nickel. We were silent. Is there like, like."

"I like you. Tell me who you are, your name please," she said.

"An appetite can only be so well to someone truly satisfied and happy," Boris said. "Her little sis always was laughing at some joke. We tried to find green mantis' praying on a leaf dark green like plastic plants. Her sis spotted one. A swarm of mosquitoes just then spotted on her brow. She could not see. I pointed it out to her. She was too small too. Right, I slapped the mosquito drinking on her face and she almost cried. I was so, so sad."

He found the world of ideas was the most dangerous place he could be. Often he put himself in the most dangerous situations. He'd step toe to toe with a gun-that carnival act candle in the wind was the flux of rainbows. He'd respond to gestures. He was walking on air. He hung up the phone.

"Shut the door!" Margery yelled to her mama; "I can't have you look on me with those dead eyes! Shut it!"

"Margery did you tell her yet?" Zoë wanted to know.

"No."

"You goin' to, ever? You've missed your period! Twice!" Zoë repeated.

"No, never." Her mother was no longer tapping short Morse code at the latched door. Zoë set a pot on to boil. "Lonnie wanted me to stop laying with other men and rolling around on the floor with them."

"Zoë, as if he could not take a hint. I'd swallow cough syrup, grape." A cough came through the transmitter wire.

"Like your his mother! He wants you to have something tugging at your cuffs."

"He's sorry, afraid they're only words, only words mean nothing," Margery said in an excited state the color drained from her; Deidra did not see, only heard; she listened to her mother's footprints faded patter behind the insulation.

"To hell with your little sis, she wants to write love notes to the son of Boris, fine," Deidra said to let off her steam beside Margie on the phone.

"It's exploitation," Margery said. Her mother's ears planted firmly listened through the panel.

"There's an April mother's day," Zoë said, "It's like an April fools, or a Saint Patrick's. Mothers who drink gin have their daughters prepare vodka in bed. Or vodka drinkers have white urine in a can. The mother scotch-whiskey drinkers get an off brand, cheap knock-offs; instead of Jameson are served Jack Daniel's."

The tape reel Mike 'N Ike could wrap his finger around a thousand and then some. "I never learned to read," he told Rudy over the phone whose voice on the copper electric tape wheel relapsed in the locked vaults of never reviewed manuscripts compiled the stripping of the corrugated wires in the human brain. He cased the houses.

"It's a shame, world," Rudy wanted to impress his ignorance at base to show he was no better than anyone else. "What a shame, mankind. War's cruel."

"It's her sister killed immediately, the car you hit," Mike 'N Ike said.

"That's terrible. Terrible." Rudy said accusingly. He had an emptied one. "I get my ideas in the car. It's the contrast rolling, the rocking motion sets my soul. It's where I sit with the passing flora. I see the signs on a road only in glimpses. The billboard-sized signs display a little girl as of yet not ten swimming donated nine of her organs. Died, as an organ donor saved nine."

"Like punching the slide projector," answered Mike, "one shot. Don't fret."

"I see the pics roll one over," Rudy said. "I'd shoot straight through the cemetery."

"See it's end up," Mike said, "like boxing the ears of rabbits, the tortoise and the hare's faster, you'll leap. Better than go over a little slower."

"There's a ship of guns coming in New York's money's scare dare cops," he said the television's satellite blaring the news report.

"Tell the tale and no shaking," he stared to his knees, said in a thick dialect of ebonics' latin, a soft talker vowels stuck on the tongue, consonants scattered in his throat. "There's a jar of standing water."

"The cat's like to lick," Rudy laughed. "You'll have to come here you want to hear."

"Then wham," Mike N' Ike said, "two-by-fours on the varmint. Hard science. Hafta stop the truck before the thud."

"Who, she?"

"No," Mike said coyly winking in the phone. "We'll see you next poison's eve." He hung up his phone in the car.

"Of Christian Charity the world knows nothing of giving," Mike spurned heavily the empty dial tone. "To hell with the fucks! Those tempters of the divine deserve it. They are the destroyers. Mess with the secret government, the civil servants eavesdrop on your boring, dull existence. It's a self-fulfilling prophecy, the vicious cycle the hooligans instigate. There's the wallpaper," he said in solitude, "hit it if he wants. Bang on it. We've torn down the third wall; we put up the fourth; we are the fourth!"

A blind street violinist caught the stench in the breeze, circulated the rumor his candy brand's name.

No one knew where he was. He signed a traveler's cheque valued at six thousand to become an essayist with the thought to dispose of dead bodies in the harbor place. No place like the water. The wind in the sails on murky weather a smell of the dead rotting stuff in the slag as sordid guts floating questions in the brine sunk to the appetites of fishes in the red iron. The sun broke in his window. On an astigmatism through the clouds the telephone receiver stared up; he saw into the dial with eyes cross. Is it the same end? The sailed fins swam in circles.

"Whine'd she cut her hair, Sue," Boris asked into the darkness, darkness moves. Off centeredness pulls him along a divergent plane.

"Sue, the daughter of a single parent had a dream she was a bear chasing the man on the moon. He was the moon-man. He went to the golf course with her, her swing had a straight shot. She was a swinger. With a lot of boys. Her swagger earned her a sore reputation. One jealous love struck boy ran after her with a golf cart once. There were bolts chiseled into her spine. Her walk was never sexier."

"Some people it don't make no difference," Dolly said. "To my son-"

"She wanted someone," Diane went on saying, "wrote letters to a holy reverend and he wrote to her, her seedlings sprouted what the scriptures neither could hear nor see, well, for his learning. He was old with weak eyes, glaucoma had thinned his sight. She'd say be kind to her glaucoma friend, sincerely. Her friends must have thought it some joke. A dream of animals she spoke to sometimes. Her boy then told her he had 'love pillows' cat's hump. He's stupid."

"Would he hurt her?" Dolly asked. "I heard he was a roughneck!"

"There was an accident," Diane said and politely told the mother of the son she may have to remove from his family, that she had to go.

He was an idiot, a perfect fool. He was a misdemeanor until he was into this band after the meters Diane recognized when she went over playing on the sound system loudly through the door. He's not so tough. A solid tone kept processing over the wiretap. He's a softy. He's only a boy, hafta remove from his parents. Then a murmur. Just the same one more complaint filed through the system. A grumble.

The sun flagged a bright fine like a bullet on the stream that had the mines' runoff the red iron ore. Sue stood through the country trailer house screened of crab grass on mud flats.

Step 6

Beneath the cabin floors in the woods with legs held up on stilts in the crawly space wresting the bugs in the leaves with a broomstick. The shadows in the deep green lake gave cover to the swimmers shadows below the water. The weight of a penny pulled at the swimmers' toes colder in the shade of the floating raft propped on round buoys and the deep shadows crept in the dim refractions, light afloat dream matter. Microcosms lit up organisms beneath the swimmers' feet in a depth deep as the stars in the sky, as the summer campers bent dripping water from the pool up the ladder. Margery and Boris sat on the stranded island in the lake aboard the rafters. The silent choir sung below the algae. The luminous glow of jelly fish lit up the lake. A motor boat skimmed the forest on the waves to float the couple to the docks. The other swimmers' had long gone. The campers had chores, mainly to sweep the mice in the dark niches under the main awning. A scary creak infested with bugs, spoiled with rain soaked into the cold mud cakes. That summer Margie and Boris were the last to the camp cabin.

"It's a place I went to be safe. No one's tagged. No one except for Lon. He went by the stream with me when it seemed a river. The water was amazingly clear. I'd puff on a phony cigarette," Boris said describing a hang-out a few streets from his girl's house on the corner miles from where she'd lived before moving.

The ticketed parked cars with yellow envelopes beneath windshields, a precursor to the hooligans hanging out in empty parking lots, held an important discussion. The speeding tickets Arty got pulled over for made him into an icon for the boys. He was a year older and never arrested before his accident, mouthed off.

"Cops are dogs. I get a ticket for being all turned around the wrong direction. They're moving in the wrong direction," he said beneath the copse of trees in the summer. He drove a silver Mazda with a dented fender beam. "Soon as everyone learns the law's impotent," he said with a forced articulation, almost sounding im-por-tant. "When you get tickets, you'll know you've been called," he laughed, "omnipotent. I looked at the phone number. It really makes you wonder whose on the other end?"

"Like you're getting the run around," Boris said, turning the conversation to car chases. Lon drove before he was fifteen, the boys were thirteen. Arty drove faster than the traffic cops.

In the bright heat swarmed the chaotic rattle of bugs, a buzzing in the rain-soaked grass. There was the strange shared thought between them no-one ever came here. No-one. "The Toyota's a fast automobile," Lon said. "And it gets fast, faster than most."

"I was speeding on the freeway one hundred and forty miles per hour," Arty said, "and no one stops in the dead of the night. There's no one out there. It's awful quiet, except for the engine."

"What if it's just the car door?" Boris asked.

The hooligans sat for hours, smoking cigarettes, staring at the sun. In the coming years the windshield glare made blind drivers on the mad highway. Boris' pride was injured. Lon made the contest to drag race to assuage the loser. For Sue, Boris agreed, or he did for Margery. He felt slightly cut off like a reckless driver passing on the right bruises the fender by a side swoop.

His naivety was loud with tact. He gave his name, never the listing in a telephone book. He did not exist outside of a paper birth certificate. He always spoke with a haughty knowledge about everything. He could tell nothing without revealing something of himself. This made him smile, but to everyone else he was smirking.

"When's the wedding?" Art asked.

"I'll never marry, no," Boris said.

"The trick is it isn't the rich red tobacco mud," Lon said, "it's poison. The difference if I drink every last brain cell to dust, I'll still want to think and believe in the human."

Boris dreams a new girl before the night. Newspapered sheets torn from the pages flutter fall out windows, the confetti ripped loose on crumbling dry wall come undone, unglued paper mache losing shape. The substance soluble in water turns into sludge. The boots make muddy tracks stumbled off the highway to sleep in the flowers. The car bolted to the shoulder on a scenic stretch, a road away from the turnabout. The grass in the yellow moon pushed through the dirt the past his hand on a clod for a pillow. The night black and blue light in the trees with the hollow sound of a river arched his narrowed neck to the flow of the water. The micro bacteria swam in the muck. He awoke restless, a dream which keeps dreams hidden even from himself.

Sue was the Saint he wanted her to be, a virtuous maiden, an angel chiseled in limestone, a broomstick bundled straw to scare the crows with a hat to seem personable. The trailers in the hay bales smolder in the sun, roll in the wind, the rake tore dry forked grass into split endings. The lonesome dispersed people in the acres of corn in a row had a rustic kindness. The abandoned communes across miles of farmland had asynchrony in the city's boarded tenement housing with a few staggered specks in the star guise.

Sue kindled her novelettes instead of trudging through heavy novels preferred the new lighter variety, anything had to be digital worth it's salt. The archaic turned her nose skyward. He had to squint on a text the size of his hand, he'd never unfold those baggy monsters. He saw her unkindly in the bathtub with her kindle sliding in an execution electrocution. He tried hard to visualize a grain of sea salt, only a speck in the windshield glare.

The camp in the summer at the beach, the swimmer sunk below the green, salty water, the undertow struggling his heels to the Atlantic. The salt stung his nose mucus yet he went under to the intermutable space beyond thrown in the waves to hold his air in a puffed trunk. The camp guard stood on the shore, unsure and unassured he was a learned swimmer. Only a boy no one knew swirling his feet through the invisible nets and fishing lines. When he pulled himself in the counselor shook his beard, "no, 'd stay out of the ocean."

Boris laughed at the other campers. To mock him they had floated a raft into the deep. The boys fought to keep afloat. To board the inflated tree-shaped floating logs tied with twine, knocking into bare, naked skin with a waxy-white sheen, splashing into the white riptide with arms twisting like insects.

"How's that look," the counselor said in a foreboding tone.

"Gay," Boris said laughing and he couldn't stop laughing despite serious and officious glares. He was never so mad to leave yet when the time came he was ineffectual to most everyone.

Sometimes Borisovich's house was cold like Poland. The door's on a fragile hinge, silently squeaking. It's mostly unlocked. The deadbolt's broke. Everyone on the block can pass through freely. No one wants to, so hooligans head wherever by cement square on the stoop where his tree, the one he had, everyone has a tree-his is yellowing under the leaf; it's just tough to snap the branch with a sinewy green strand in the wood; he had to feel unaware so all know the heart rests in every one.

"If he hands you a roach, don't draw smoke," Lon said about his friend Jerry.

Lon's friend the film student, he's never belonged to a film school but calls himself director. He's a neo-Nazi punk. Jerry's profile stuck in Boris' mind. He had a perfectly shaved head with Boris grandfather Ivan's LP's sorted in no particular order against the wall-length three-tiered shelves. He must have thought Boris' taste refined. The records weren't even Boris'. He'd no inclination to satisfy Jerry's interest in J.S. Bach Preludes.

"I had this dream, maybe you can tell me what it means," Jerry said. "You seem like someone who knows that sort of thing. I was with this girl and she was drop dead gorgeous. I had to do her. She says I have to wear a rubber. So I get this feeling I have to get out of there to the convenient store down the street, only it's taking forever to get there. I keep running but I never seem to get there."

"Darius, Darius," teased the eighth graders in the locker-room with a long us. His penis matured early for the seventh graders. He's take pride in the showers with his new piece. He bent over his rotund, plump belly to gander at his dick.

"Darius Milhaud," the boys laughed. Rudy, red Rudy, the eighth graders teased. He'd get so red. Rudy Panko, one man's son called him. Where do children learn the names of narrators and the avant- garde?

The tough muscle cord in a ring he tore at darned red-striped socks pulling at the fabric stretched and torn in his larger hands. He was small as a sparrow the thought before he barely had the words to chirp. He took the gift from the old fellow with poor near-sightedness, Pop, while he had no cloth on his foot, and knew the material he clasped was cotton, unthreads, wool holds better.

The muscle attracted Rudy as he stared across the street behind the tinted glass in the car parked by the liquor store. The white star repelled. Jerry stumbled in the street with ears full sounding stuffed with feathers, his matted hair stuck from the pillow standing with head ducked between his heels underwater. He had a reoccurring plot to make into a movie. A sniper who picks off only the ignorant, and he'd spend thirty pages he'd already wrote about the sniper and his intense mind frame, spent barely a thought on the targets.

"He soft her," Mike slurped in a register compliant with blank verse. "The desk claire 'k."

"Handle on the wagon. Little juicy fellon the chair toenail's the cup," Jerry said rambling in incoherent Baltimorese,

"Cut 'in the numb uh over that ways," Mike said assumingly.

"Got blest her da law'd we ther gawd an' thorn prick the thing her. Ah miss'd her," a gold grin shone in a broke salutation.

"Ives a trick trough, ma jick'd," the hand had a sleevefunnel newspaper in a waterglass, "git me aghast of water. Ah no mind," he said, "'t git you sum."

The ink smeared on the pages as the water pours and he dragged the unbreakable cup which snapped on concrete. "There's no broke."

"He laugh'd him."

"He's laugh'd her," Jerry's gold mouth said, "he was call'd in the nose. Hoola gelatin th' tin man?" his teeth were ground finer than coffee.

"Ther's stole nun," Mike held a magazine with an infamous dictator smoking a stogee, "that's sum gun."

"He got a greek deaf."

"He sane of left an eye aint lyin' uh forum. 'e cant ear nun a raise a fifth one cut of fit," Mike said to

Rudy's shadow having took his car with the intent to drive away.

"Old sammy pulled a racing pistol from 'dis gig," he showed a racing pistol prop. "ther's a blank in a one!"

Jerry and Mike were in hysterics. Rudy chose voluntary exile and wrote a letter not to someone famously admired even as he was inclined to do because he might get a letter, but to the stink bags, a city gang at war warning to steer away of him and his automobile because he'd had enough with setting fires to family flats, th' slash-and-burn, Sherman polemic-when he got home wasted.

Boris' car sped ninety miles per hour. He could go no faster. He could almost see her before him. The leaden clouds were heavy in the overcast sky. The dusty vinyl discs wrapped in plastic on a shelved wall had clogged his nose. The car swerved capsized on the road, twelve steps to the car from the ground had he a breath to take he'd breath in the dirt. The jaundiced grass paler in the sun than in the rain.

Boris Ivanovich invested in houses, refurbished the old brick. Land rent was up, the homeowners could not pay the cash for the tenant could not pay in June, the mortgage was due and in September the offer was made to buy a home. Evicted the same week she sang the blues.

Ain't got no money
ain't got no money
ain't got no money
gonna sue your mother

Lease has ran out
can't pay the rent
lease has ran out
can't pay the rent
Pleanty of lead

taken the stove
refrigerator
took the stove
made out of gas

my little girl's sick
little girl's sick 'n ill
sicker than dead
gotta move outta town

Step 7

The waves in the ocean to the banks on the shore, under the cobblestones, there is a block of brickwork, where there are waiting for a fourth, people. Bricks blush by the street lamps. A shop-front painted white with blue stripes over faces the ocean. The flight of seagulls in the dark sky and watery in the wind ripples to the wooden pier. Fiery bricks pave the grounds, an island in an island between parallel streets. The block an island to the block previous is an island to blocks before that, brick islands. Standing three-sided people in the brick island, they await under the wet, moist air for the final nightcap.

On the other block was a woman by the fountain on an island. She was sitting on stone. A man was sitting by the tavern. The tabby passed the man walking beside the wall, snuffed its pink nose. The man snorted. Then he grumbled. Homelessly walking with his hands folded out uncomfortably in a stupor.

Sleeping fenced in the shadows of the stone in blue and green a man walks beside the homeless with a leaning gait. The man with denim and white was behind him and the third was walking beside him. The first was closest and put a dime in the cup. The homeless man mumbled under his breath something. He was drowsy and stares at the sailing boats. Floating in the bay, the flying gulls in the air and the mice scratching on the docks. Fish were bubbling in the water. The ocean seems for the moment to be sleeping. The movement of the waves beneath the piers on the bright lights of the lamps and the moon and stars on the water. Shadows on the nights' shadow. The moon streaks the water and passing clouds in a haze of blues and purples flask in shady gray masses of cloud over the green ocean. The moving on sleeted pavement under the sallow glow of lamps, were moving as the homeless man saw motions on the oceans' cobbles. The homeless snored the damp air through a nose slow silent breaths as the waves rolled beneath. His eyelids slowly close as he slept. The lights from the coffee shops beam through the windows on the door stones. As the lights melt into shadowy darkness slowly breathing seemed to inhale the entire ocean from the bay like a drowning man dragged to the piers only to depart and watching at the shorelines. The street lamps' glowing orbs shone on lining an orb after the sidewalks turn and they are gone. Clicking heels shuffle clothes silently moved in the air. Crosswalks and red and green lights flashing red, then green. Leaning, the homeless man faces the water and water moving beneath the piers, silently squirming fishes under the water, the moon on matchless sky and the light in the foggy bay.

The bum pressed his fingers at the gray between the concrete squares against the shadowy red brick row houses and bright street lamps, snoring.

Over the street there is a boy dancing barefoot on the asphalt. On the street with pieces of broken glass in blue plastic bags: blues, yellows, reds, greens and orange. "Blues," he says.

"Greens," the other says picking his fingers over the sharp piece of green glass from the concrete the shards. He hands the fragment as the other holds the bag so the glass can fall inside the plastic folds where there are sharp pieces of glass.

Across the street there is a man asleep against the brick, admirer of liquor bottles. They walk home. The boys are hopping on bare feet across the street and the hot asphalt is like a thick sea in the afternoon. The boy rubs with his fingers washing the glass in the sink in the soapy water. The older collects the sparkling glass in a pile on the towel at the wood table. The fragments accumulate as he pushes folded napkins in the backyard on the grass. He buries the glass when it gets dark like an animal in a grove.

Sixteen shots in rapid succession, glass shatters on the windshield blood splatters on the driver's seat, the passenger falls under the dashboard. The shooters in the loft are firing from the second floor of a house on the block. There are eight men dead. The lights go on and there is shouting.

The boy stares at the television lines and zigzags, listening to the noises of mother and father standing in the room talking in words with gestures more than sounds. The older brother in the kitchen stands with the dishwasher cycling noisily. Falls face-forward; the red and blue sirens flashing. His mother in the kitchen places her child hugging her arms. He cries for being at that place he was when he was not supposed to have been. The boy watches the TV stations fade and flurry out; listens to the dying sounds of helicopter rotating blades in the city sky as Police sirens whirl dreams of bright lurid panthers.

Louis stands at the corner of the street with the shattered cars. King drives to the curb after the police are gone and he walks in. The car drives to the street brick warehouse hiding dilettantes. They lose sight on the rattle of conversation. He walks in with a square lamp table. A man with gorgon eyes cuts powdered pills on glass with scissors. "Do you want to get cut?!"

She rubs powder on her lips and pouts. Her stockings cling to her legs and there is a tear in the wooly threads. The man with the gorgon, he eyes the girl ethereally in the flesh. He feels creepily like spiders crawling on his skin. When he shifts the lamp shivers. She looks quietly at the tiles where the carpeting has ripped. It was very dark outside. Louis walks in the dim lights at the table end beside heavy brass knobs. Posted photographs are on the wood partition. He was searching for faces he could not recognize and there was the man he knew. The figure with the black, top hat and overcoat flapping to his knees stood standing by the tart damp raining from the sky like a debutante in a lace dress. The wet weather was difficult to see in. He closes and makes sure the lock is set in the circular niche. Pushing against the handle knob, he knows he is locked in. There are ashes smoldering the sink. The faucet drips. Water runs on his hands wipes on his pants, walks down the passage and stares in the space, timeless void. The figure of a manly woman plays in his minds' eye. Her eye is a shadowy silhouette cast like puppet theater as the lamps light the walls. He closes the door.

Louis listened to the two talking while he walked out to the blue September night. The gray concrete, rushes water in the drains and rain speckling the lenses and a streak of light across the glossy glasses. There must have been a mistake. He had trouble adjusting the eyes to the light. Walking at this hour of the night, the sky was in a clearing the clouds' phlegm as the rains wash humid and damp. The planted trees from tires of the sidewalk claw like lions hiding in the den of the moon. The avid slowness of life and death was in every jitter of each step, although he couldn't feel a thing. The earth was moving faster and the harbor was not-watching the building moving towards him like the distant Jupiter or birds flapping around in the air above the storage houses near the docks! The grounds became sandy and that was how he knew the water was closer. The sand on concrete and the blue air was from the ocean winds. On the docks he was searching the buoyed water for gulls and buoys; bay weed and junk was floating in the water. He could see his reflection in the murky dyed-ink blue. The moon glowing above his atrophy glaring at him. He could see the far out, the island where he had been walking that he builds an island away from, his leaving, standing, the corner of the parking lot, brings to mind the sewing machine.

It was so he decided to leave in a train heading southbound through the rolling hills and brighter sunsets. The mysterious night on the night Police knocked at his house locked-out the night sounds softly as he was closed-in. He decided it would be best to leave the town. Walking to the train station he had to walk around a graveyard and the graves in the sunlight shine in the grassy mown flats. The black-iron fence rises from the hard cement napping on the gravestones. There is somebody on the grass. The airy morning over his ears blankets his feet. The flowers on the grass are yellow with white weed blowing from untended borders on the fence poles. The dull pounding in his temple continues with his steps to the bus stop. The bus ambles on the corner where the white top stripes visibly in the distant rocks. He boards the bus on the curb and pulls the Go Pass from the coin machine. The vehicle steers towards the buildings and houses rotate passed bumpy asphalt but the bus awkwardly breaks. The south train leaves in the station room. Benches line the wall beside a young woman with flaxen hair and her pleaded skirt drags to her knees. She is stunned at the benches sat back on the beige tiles and holds her purse close to her stomach swinging her legs underneath. The shuffle of passengers leaving the train. He sees she has too and boards the locomotive with her. The announcement on the speaker: all aboard! The station bell rings and he sits beside the young lady as the train starts to jump. He studies her icy and somber nose curves like a tropical birds, the flat of her lips creases and her eyes do not match. He wonders. He falls asleep in a few minutes from the lulling motion the locomotive cries and carries him until he forgets about the trip. There is a slight ache in his shoulder and he elbows the woman sitting beside him with his tiredness.

The note was stapled to the table in his morning delirium undertaking a momentous conjecture that the great men rise not out of determination, but are predetermined by their names. In the train is a man with his tongue stuck in his teeth and snoring through the buttons on his shirt. His cravat catches on his shirt right over his belt loop the buttons on his jacket are turned slightly askew. He has hair hanging down too far over on the leftward part and sideburns are untrimmed low with legs over legs on the seat, stares forward at the signs. On his brows is handsome beige hair seeming slightly frizzier than the hair on his head, eyelashes on eyes. The runaway tilts his head and stares at the rough edge of trees disappearing and changing in the blurry, gray rocks. Louis spoke in a delirium between dream and sleep. The train stopped, he did not hesitate at whatever station there was. There came a long, low bemoaning sound in his ears like the breath blowing through the ram's horn echoing in the wet pools of his wakefulness in the station. With a clatter and a din scuffle of his shoes on the checkered slippery floors. His shoes were wet from mop water. He nodded as she waited for him to stand on his feet and lean towards the door, his shoes squeaking on the water. He leans on her shoulder on the ride home and is quiet and no longer cognizant of the things going on. He wakes up beside her naked silhouette in quilted bed sheets in the bedroom. Her nipples on soft skin. On her naked body flat against her. Breasts had been removed from her by a paring knife. Her clothes draped over the blue carpet, yellow wallpaper and beige ceiling and she had rich lips. He stares at the wallpaper. The peeling shapes have pictures other than what were. The storm shook the houses with an angry stroke of thunder and lightning. Sleep was taking hold of Henri while he was sitting at the table across from their guest. Ida was standing beside the stove as fire was burning with quiet intensity. Sat at the table with his hand resting on the bare shoulders of her black dress. Ray was the name of the guest as he introduced himself at their door moments earlier. He was a friend of Lou. He was walking nearby and thought would become better acquainted with them. The rain was damp. Water on his shoes dripped to the wood floor and then Ray apologizes.

"There is no problem," Ida says. "These floors have had water drip on them before. There are steps leading from an alley that are a waterfall for rain. I put boards over the steps but water seeps through then leaks underneath the door. There is sawdust which soaks water the floods."

"I am vulgar dripping water over the place," Ray says. "I was just going home when I must have taken a wrong turn and here I am, a friend of your friend, wherever he is."

"Away," she says, "That's what you might say about him."

Ray says, "doesn't have much weight though. He has a lot of talk and nothing behind his ears that give legs, so he just sits."

"He has a hearing condition. He's got a bad ear and a bad eye on his left side," Henri says.

"What do you call that," she says, "Fluids are in the ear, his ears are full with bees."

The gas burner glowed with a blue flame on the kitchen stove with a copper pan on with glossy liquor settling in the pan. A bitter wind howling against the screen wires sent a shiver down her back. The waling cats whistle with the storm and the gassy aroma hissing the sound of the steady flame on the burner stove. Wet water drops on the brick stair as she steps out in the sleek rain under the shingles onto their porch. Pale, bright eyes are in starry darkness bustles and depart. She is soporific with the hissing of fire boiling the liquor wakes her as she steps in to pour the whiskey into a shot with an ice cube that melts liquor, makes the whiskey watery warm. "Wake up," Ida says to Henri who was falling asleep in his chair.

"Was about to ask," Henri says reveling, "somewhere you think he has gone. I admit it seems worrisome when spoken like that."

Ida is startled by the words almost spilling liquor as she walks across the room and puts the glass down. She is nervous about the sounds outside and she imagines the dangerousness of streets and of sidewalks. Ray drinks from his glass. There is a fat cat sleeping comfortably on the floor silently watching in the sharp corner while Ida stands beside the burning stove. Ray sits in his seat and warms his sleeves.

"Too cold," she says.

"Windy when you open up the house," Henri says.

"Thought I heard something outside that turned out to be nothing," she says. Ida leaves the room to get a sweater and scarf on the unusually cold evening while the storm throws rivulets of rain on the roof. Pouncing Henri hears the gallop of hoofs on the far-off horizon and envisions the conquerors passing over the Alps riding on golden-saddled elephants. He sees the bright, ivory tusks appearing on the cloudy mists and white snows and the droning march of the Carthaginians led by great hopes that have led so many elephants across the Alps to surprise helpless armies. There must have been fortresses. Labyrinthine cages one of those elephants with enormous hoofs and shiny tusks are to know. The enemies army would be caught unawares by something so huge, bright, Henri sees as the rain pounding on the shingles and draining in the water pipes in the flush of the gutter drown out, and stars flash in the black. The speck of flint on the lighter sparks a cigarette Ray's fingers. Ray seeping with quiet anger and crouching like a lion grips the whiskey glass. There is a knock on the door. The light of red and blue, police sirens. The flashes in the dark through the glass window. The knocking gets louder.

"What can I make of that?" says Henri. "We are where he is and hope he finds what he is looking for. Do you understand me?"

"Hey officer," Andrew greets the Police and steps outside. The door closes behind him. The rain splatters on the marble in blots off-white on white. In the kitchen methamphetamine are on the stove sizzling.

"Carthaginians?" Ray asks in a loud voice.

"They were hero conquers across the mountains. Have you ever seen the Alps?" Henri asks.

"Have I seen a mountain?" he says with emphasis. "Yes."

"Are you looking for it?" Henri asks, "Red-necked goose!"

"And if I were?" he asks.

"There were Carthaginians," Henri says.

"Red!" he says.

"Drunk!" Henri says.

"And I do not care for your patriotism," Ray says angrily pushed forward from his seat and stood lumbering. He was over a foot taller than him and standing.

"Are you serious?" Henri asks. "You might crush me."

"You take that back!" he shouts.

"Are you looking for it?" Henri asks and sat comfortably in his chair.

"That's it!" Ray shoves and punched square in his eye knocking him out of his chair. He cries out and hurries out of the room. "Who do you think you are?" he says and walks into the Police outside of the house. The Police officer began writing a report for a missing person.

The policeman asks, "What was all of that noise?"

"It's nothing," Henri says and snatches his fingers at the air of his attacker standing in the hall through a crack in the door. "You red neck!" he hollers. "You've a lot of nerve smacking your host! You've what is coming to you, I hope you get it!" stands in the street hollering beside the car and shouts at the house. "If I were you, you wouldn't hit someone your height, you broke!" The police had the attacker in iron wrists shackles the police car. The suspect glares mumbling as rain falls on oily streets and runs in rivers.

Step 8

Isaac and Ray were brothers. He took a knife and cut his hand, and Isaac cut his. They split matches in half to light cigarettes in cold hands warmed in the noxious smoke. "Reds" Ray asked for. "Mediums," Isaac said, and he would ask for lighter tar smokes before his moving away from Ray's drag.

Ray's were too wild, and he was smoking unfiltered. The smoky cars driving in the icy weather sliding on snowy streets in blurry, flaky nights with street-lights emblazoned on glassy snow. He saw through the bars smoky air. The black square floor with shifting feet sliding on slippery rubber to florescent pink lights, skating on the sidewalk before the cover cost at the unhinged gate. The wet chafer slides over watery gin. Drinkers drink ice water sound proof in the singing bar. The freezing weather shrinks Ray's cherry's on his cigarette papers, sitting beside Loda like the ghost got him, the tobacco warming his fingers, fills his lungs with gaseous smoke, inflating and deflating like a balloon. He falls beside her already drunk.

He has his hand on hers, and she walks off with him. He stares with cold eyes, and she hardly sees him. The fatty muscles clinging to his bones already coagulate oily, black ink, and night spouts like an inkwell. It's a temperate day when Isaac walks in the medical clinic to see his physician. He has receipts from the bakers' to prove his coverage and signs a medical log book to tab his visits.

The waiting area has magazines on the table with poems, news and popular culture. His stomach turns as the pages flip sticky pages. "I.S.," the receptionist calls.

"Dr. will see you," she says. The cold office walls are as sterile as the metal beds with torn cushions. The white fluorescent light is blank on the white floors, on the white, blank walls and the sawdust desk.

"Please have a seat," the Dr. says. She has short brown hair, and appears in her late 40s wearing medium glasses on her slightly aging face.

"I've also been feeling dizzy with hallucinations. My left eye worsens. When I walk, my thighs lean. I leave water boiling, which worries me. The metal makes noises - water boiling. It's not supposed to," Isaac says. She performs tests on his fluids and returns with a response, his results. "There is a carcinoma in your liver, the test reveals," she says.

The city was dark and the asphalt was shivering wet with rain. Rats were on the cold tarred streets scurrying under the blue-paint, wood stairs from the brick and wood boards with claws scratching the rough sidewalk with chalk lines. Of the names of rats who had been clearly on the leaves on the limbs of trees philander in the square a tryst of shadows on the figures in the loose night clinging to the branches. Rustling with the scratchy, high-pitched echo in the heated canals of the ear bone, the stoned stairs are glistening with marble. The loosely drawl time between autumn and summer nestles by the stores, buildings boarded-up over windows broken-in on the row, of a rat pictured the ocean harbor contemplating the depths, blue white-mouthed water washing brick. The rain washing over cracked holes and drainage vents in the concrete running clots of hairy thickness scraping dissolution against the red brick walls flowing on the drag. Windswept gutters and rain pipes along the roofs of houses pouring on the sidewalk, the chimney shoot dark smoke fluff from the pipes like pigeons, sparrows and bats.

Swaying limbs to leaves with long hooked fingernails and birds' caws, rats dangling like apples. Rats struggled in the canopy falling on the grass, splashing on the strands of dew-dappled grass like into a sea of emerald and garnets. Rats set fires to strips of newspapers that brightened the garden bright orange and yellow. Lugubrious cigarettes were rolled like tulips from newspapers resting on the rocks in the garden as rats puffed-out stomachs with tobacco smoke. The first of several spit into the flames as the fires spit newspaper, burnt newspaper scattering on the grass. Flapping wings birds' leaping from the ferns with talons, squirming gray bodies with peppering feet pouring red wine from tall bottles to round white saucers, the crimson wine splashes against teacups filling saucers to the brim and splashing red. Teacups tip over the balance of rats. Silvery forks shine and knives, gripping birds, rats feasting on sparrows, crows and saucers fly jacked 'neath wet paws. Teacups pummeling noses cracking stacks of bowls toppling to pieces, glass chipping from the paws and broken with the weight of pouncing rats' pidgin cooing on the windows flapping in the canopy of trees, the sparrows shuffling, rats hiding in the shade. Rough fragments of shaved shapes scamper against the side of the house into a hole in the roof of the attic. In the watery deafness, birds fly. The harbor is a mirror. Tears shed in the solemn glowering moon on water painting, King Louis XIV. The crystal palace floating in the warbling wet circles of the eyes like ice in water glasses as the rats march along the parapet on the grassy park. Seagulls flapping wings and the sparkling moon red in the eyeglass. Breathlessly light movement of dancers washed in gullets tightly wound belts and swift bated breaths, black tuxedo pants, frilly shirts, clicking buttons which chafing, burning swells worn elaborate belle dresses; silky satins, crimson and lace corsets around the thinning waists disappearing in the machine, of the time-telling clock. Cars steered from the alleyway to the street and parked on a corner. Car lights fiery like cats' eyes and rats were crawling from gutters; sprouting heirloom tomatoes, eggplants, sage and basil, grass beneath the shade of an apple tree; sparrows and crows on the extended branches like arms reaching for forbidden fruits; the rats pattering like crows frowning with beaks pecking rustling mites, ants, cockroaches.

The broom handle hits the ceiling the mice in the attic running around in circles foot pattering on wood and the broom lowered from the wood and put down on the couch as if it were a rifle with ammunition. On the ledge of the window are clear bottles of vodka, teacups with moss growing dripping white blood with drying leaves, blue carpet; the cat moans stretching her paws with silvery gray muzzle. The alarm rings, the radio broadcasts and with the cat in his arms shifting the creature to the bed and slipping shoes on his feet, out of bed, from the linens another cat stares.

The light cord hung limpid on the ceiling. Flicking the wall the room became bright. The dreary gloom of the day shone entered through the window with the dastardly smell of gray and dismal rain. The wet placid rain and the turning light bulb left a silhouetted cat and the sunlight filtering on the ledge. Outside, the street runs like a river flowing on the rolling hills.

Creaking footsteps on the flight of stairs, newspaper on the kitchen table before the day and the day before. He turned the burner on the stove to boil the tea in the kettle. The teacup on the news article shifts a wet ring covered the moisture over the type. Sipping tea room-temperature soaks four spoons of diluted sugar. The sleeper folds pages reading inside the teacup ring with a cat on the newspaper. He folds the paper from behind the weighty cat, staring with golden green eyes, silently. The sleeper quacks sulking at the black and white kitchen tiles and the ledge on the tablecloth spread-out and the shadow on the table in the light looks like the flicker of a candle flame.

Sleepwalking to the brick steps, the sleeper walks outside through a screened door and sits on the step sipping tea as a cat wandered to his foot. Moving through the garden was a cat in the leaves hissing, the thistles on the thyme shuffle with the silent stalker. Dahlias grow on the ledge along a cat slithers in the grass; the sky was humid. Calico cat behind the dahlias; a cat jumps into the street while behind the calico watches the sleeper furtively behind the flowers sip tea; watery, the sun is hot in a sea of wet clouds and the heavy air in the branches of the apple trees, leaning over the masonry and sheltering irises.

The kettle whistles. Taking a sip, every minute: a sip; stop, a sip, a sip, and listens to the heating vents' purr with the cat lost inside which whiskers' flicker stuck on the newspaper. The chair scrapes the kitchen floor as he gets up from the chair and walks to the other room, the teacup simmering. He walks out on the marble steps, the sidewalk on the store the corner of Miracle. The cant awakening along brick houses, he hums to a song he cannot remember only with two of the notes remaining, which he considers an odd note. The windy weather tastes bitter from copper-tasting tea, PG tips in the stale tea water and the sunshine lackadaisically under the leaves tremble airily over the sloping street and brick. He has a paper note torn from the daily newspaper. He walks into the Miracle on the block, and sits at the end of the barstool watching the pouring drinks.

Shapely in a rectangular shoebox where the fat Henri was resting his hand heavy as a pistol on the square table, eating a glossy pear pretty as a painting with a bowl of fruit and a clown with shirt half-hanging out of his loose belt loop in canvas slacks. He examines the paper note in the tight fist of the man at the drinking table whose head is in his hands flat pressed against elbows on the ledge. All of the things that Henri eats, chickens with feathers stewed in bubbling hot grease sapping marrow in brewing stock pots. There is an item he drinks coffee with butter where the waitress arrives carrying a rattling tray with a silver pitcher and cups and sets them on the table pouring steamy water from the pitcher; they bubble over in the cups.

The bartender is watching the colors on the television set while the sleeper is at the counter synesthetically listening to the sound shapes. He has the drive stronger than a recruitment posters' red, white and blues. Uncles Sam needs you.

"We are the dry cleaners," Henri speaks softly into the bubbles in the smug words he can muster.

"We have the bullets, yet we have no gun," the sleeper gestures at the stool on the ledge, if only he had the iron and the patents, his hands would hold him. He stood up from the table and walking across the dimly lit shop outside from behind the register sat the shop owner quietly listening in; the light outside the door flashes through the dim light; and he was gone! The waitress walks to the table carrying a silver tray with porcelain pitcher and cups, the folds of her blue dress, shifting with her slender form and she drops in her chair, tosses three sugar cubes into the fat man's teacup; he has nothing.

"Hey," Henri says into his hands. "You want the cup of tea?"

There were four, copper pennies shining beneath the sun on the marble stairs by the concrete on the flat engraving the taste of copper in his mouth; he had fled blindly with shadows from the leaves, swaying in a familiar way of walking; there was always a stale taste of copper from his morning tea.

The brick buildings heat in the sun as the light shines through murky gray mists; vacant windows stare from across the streets. The sky on the rooftop enclose the square. The sloping pavement and the walk traces down and up along an incline half-circling topsy-turvy awaiting to hear. He thought about whom she was. Her flowery figure vanished as he walked further down the block; beside him grass went by, he counted the squares of the sidewalk near the street-side gardens, the trees growing in holes dug down cement, recognizing cracks in the sidewalk, errs strange and the slopes on the asphalt and street. He picked a flower from the dirt.

Four pennies on the marble slab staring at the roofs of houses across the street, the copper shimmers on the white marble slab, the sun through the cloud on the stairs and the brick. The funeral procession for an officer shot. The cars ride the street but along main roads through the city and through the housing bricks and the wooden fences. On the other side of the street there are two men walking. The middle of the road bumps to a small hill in the center and the asphalt is cracking with the heat of the sun. There are four cars on the curb. There are six steps from the street to the stairs and five steps to the brick houses. In the living room, there is a glass window facing a brick wall with doily-yellow drapes, daisy prints and the glass vase on the windowsill, paint chipping from the banister where the flower will be in the vase.

Louis spits on the pieces of glass bottles beneath the leathery soles broken into tiny shards like sparkling grains. Sunlight reflects the shards emerald as ocean water on the oceans shattering waves sparkling on the raining, gray pavement. Crossing from concrete corner to concrete corner, the gutter sparsely with trash washes the rains along the curbstones. Bottles glimmer in the sunlight window displays in the vacant sign in blank lettering: WONDERLAND PHARMACY AND LIQUORS: 5:00 a.m. to 10:30 p.m. CLOSED. Houses with brick and marble stairs wave across the street, trees growing on squares towards the sky shaking limbs wet with rainy, watery drops.

A Toyota parks beside the curb with a plastic bag over the shards from a stone put through disappearing inside the transparent reflection and the glare of the sunlight on the glass. The reflection in the glass slides him off the transparent window like a shadow on the earth. The stranger holds the box on the ground and a duck waddles. "I want to leave," Louis says. "There were oysters."

"Those are ducks' shit! No one promised you anything."

"Nobody wants rotting oysters. They left without their houses. Seems as though the wind would lift the houses right off this block."

"Snails," the stranger says. "Can you spare some change, we're trying to get some food at the Chicken Shack." He is smoking Camels.

The duck in his hands, the Oldsmobile with Louis in the passenger seat with a trail of duck feathers floating around the ankles. There is a chain-link fence with wire. Barking wet eyes. Louis was quiet closing his eyes and falling further in his seat to arrive in a dream, air rises and the cloudy air on the watery glass, glaring brightly from the floundering sun. It seems the pull of the automobile along the street turn on back streets; the passing houses merge into a solid formation and the morning in the city is warm while drops on the windshield splatter and the wipers sloshing water slowly blurs into hills, buildings vanish in the shield like sails in a fog.

Step 9

Sunken eyes with soft skin, and a small beard stands counting the latex condoms in the supermarket. The Jew in a tallis he totters at with fingers at the shelves on the prices listed beneath the latex condoms. Condoms, -oys, the cost is bankruptcy.

The women at the supermarket, the girls are slightly perked with his inspection. He has a sharp desire for a banquet, a feast. The unnumbered merchandise falls in the basket with salami and rye outweighing the latex condoms.

The physician has condoms at no cost to the ruddy youngsters. The wastes on a red star with rowdy gangsters fill those balloons with sudsy water to drop off tall buildings. The Jew in a tallis leaves the latex condoms on the shelves because he cannot afford the cost for copulation. He prays if the girl when she sees his small beard sees him, sees her.

The Jew boy, thirteen-years-young, shopping for his mother at the grocery at the corner store was mute with the girls; the youngster was hoarse with his siblings before he had his tallis. His early morning prayers were heard through the walls in the row houses. Solid gray shouts hammered on brick mortar. He ran a flight of stairs head long and was struck dumb, long stitches sewing his eyes shut with the seamstress nurse where his head struck the linoleum; walking out of the kitchen with the sight of a young blond chick, the Jew boy, explains with silent sighs.

The chick with golden locks is snacking on red, candied cherries. She offers a cherry candy, and the boy tastes the sugary fruit, smiles and in a brief silence, remembers the spill on the stairs and does not say anything.

Walking in the streets, the rain is falling heavier than needles with thread and the Jew in the tallis must sit on a bench watching in the rain, the wet puddles wash in the streets and the gentleman with bowed heads pushing through watery drapes counting the stars.

The Jew in the tallis keeps a close eye on the rising, yeasty bread in the ovens with an estranged discerning nose. In the morning, the loaves are scalding hot in the simmering steam out of the oven, simmering gently scraping beneath the wooden paddle on the hot brick. Max, the baker pulls the wooden pole with the paddle tossing the fresh loaves on stainless steel-grated shelves with firm hands. The tallis pulls with strings on the house ceiling, a square hat with a ladle, and Max, the baker, wares a cap; keeps curly hair from dripping sweat. The Jew's hat droops on his wet slick head and his small beard touches the crust sweating yeasty tears in his bitten fingers where the cuticles have ripped off. He pushes the loaves in a cart with the sun not yet rising to cool in the sickle-shaped moon. After the loaves are carefully wrapped, the warm bread breathes in paper wrapping and the Jew in the tallis begins to walk home with the baker, Max. There is a beggar on the road to beg, not yet working in sparse traffic. The cars' whistling like flies buzzing on a sleeping ear, slightly disturbed and in the flight shortly after the larvae. Max drives the Jew where he needs to rest, yet the hours until light are ever creeping closer, and the flour on the dry skin itches. The gnats on the flesh sting and the old veins quicken with *an ancient sadness, the joy of deep basses in chorus*. "We live short lives," the assistant explains to the baker, and in the prayers each prays shortly before the night ends, because neither will sleep soundly. The muscular aches and cracked bones bend in beds where he is tormented with ugly night visions and the bakers' pains. The Jew tosses and turns on his bedspring for hours like bread baking in the ovens on the hot stones.

Shortly before leaving to leaven the bread, there were Indian girls with short tresses, the Jew with the tallis sketched with the glint on his cornea. The glimmer on the transparent fluids with an optical enhancement on the succulent breasts in the short shadows the pall night's soft paddles had not yet scraped the supple hues. The girls' laughter on the seats

122

with buxom cheeks rosy with tranquility hardly takes note when he's stacking loaves. In hours drifting slovenly the moon runs the course and the words for the midnight prayers are not mouthed in living tongues, and the soft notes in the birds with the light chasing the dark rising on the bending trees in the lanes; the sweet apples crisp, acrid taste and the honeyed pears hard flesh, oiled with the fat sucked from a boiled chicken pot on the stove cooling on the iron coils.

The doe preparation before baking is strained with pounding, folding and creasing. In the line preparing the loaves with the Jew in the tallis fondling the gooey blobs, feeling with his fingers creased in latex gloves. With a scraper pulling the lumps on the wood boards flapping on the flour sprinkled spruce with a thump, caressing soft doe on the hard, thick table. In the sultry sweaty pulse with the slinging doe passing through the baker's hands to the plastic wrapped carts for leavening. The carts' wheels rotate in the refrigeration closets with the sliced vegetables on the wheelers. In the night mice quietly nibble on crumbs' pieces the night crew sweeps with vigorous resolve. Soap and water swashes with the mops. The squeaky wheels' pulls out of the closet for loading on the bakers' trays, sliding with a tremendous strength on a conveyer track. The loaves loosely slide on the hot stones.

"Don't hold the broom like that!" Max says. "You have to hold the handle with hands wide spread, think of holding a baseball bat, and wide strokes, dig in the dust, or there will be mice."

"I'd prefer the mice," the Jew in the tallis says, "because you can see I'm having trouble with this."

The humor was lost, as hours later when the Jew's hat was mopping in wide strokes like painting a mural on the blurry floors, Max snuck up and snapped, "No!" and took the mop and washed the suds.

The loaves bake in the ovens and the night crew washes hands and sups on bread, meats and cheese. The Jew in the tallis spoke on orgone accumulators which are tubes with the explicit purpose to harness energies. "What energies." Max asked.

"The organs have energies, all things have energies and the orgone is the unit measuring the life-giving particles; think the pull holding buckets stuck and the strength to separate those buckets is human, in the organs; the orgone are in everything," the Jew in the tallis explains.

The mice scurry in the dark and with the bakers in the kitchen, wherever the eyes cannot see, the mice thrive. The security guards walk rounds in the warehouses, and Max holds the mouse in his hands, and lets the mouse run across the cooling bread. The furry mouse skips on the loaves as a rock on a placid lake with leaves floating.

"I never knew my father," Max says, "he was Jewish. I dropped out of high school, and the girl I fell in love with is smart with a scholarship, Chicago and Baltimore, and I feel horrible trying to convince her to stay here, but that's what I'd want for her to marry me."

"Is there a difference in price?" the Jew in the tallis asks.

"Hah," Max laughs, "I was brought up by my mother, and slowly I'll buy her house from her."

"Poe was abandoned as a boy and his natural parents were a troupe of traveling acrobats, his mother was on a playbill, and she was quite breath taking," the Jew in the tallis says.

"You know many facts," Max says. "Where do you pull these things out of?" The night snacks were a daily ritual. The loaves came out of the ovens, and the Jew in the tallis had his hands full sorting bread on the stainless steel shelves. The chatting between Max, the baker and the Jew in the tallis was ritual. Out of the ordinary was when the manager Ben asked nonchalantly after the shift, if the Jew in the tallis remembered packaging shelves for Waverly. "You lost me 500 dollars!" Ben said, and the Jew in the tallis was sure he had not forgotten, yet the shop keeper on the phone said differently.

"Loda was a whore!" Max says, "I've slept with her!"

"Yes," the Jew in the tallis says, "I've heard," and the loss incurred on the business was not so great. She was an Iroquois in blood with protestant ethics thrust on her, and he was in love with her. The children would be fluent in French wines. He was deeply intoxicated with her.

There was an old racist with a telescopic lens across the street in a rickety house with the recorder pointed at the curtains across the street behind the lovers made love. The fascist was a pervert, and an eccentric old man with entertaining penchant for clowns, prostitutes and indentured servitude. The plethora made a disconcerting show for the lovers with the television set wheeled in the closet. On the television was Bart Simpson on a radio show with two priests and a rabbi Hyman Krustofsky answering the question, "if a son defies his father and chooses a career that makes millions of children happy, shouldn't the father forgive the son?" The two priests say, "I think so. Yes, of course," and Hyman shouts, "Never, never!"

The Jew in the tallis held the gold leaf on the bible at her and asked, "This is sacred?"

"Please no," Loda says, and there was no further discussion. On the couch in the evening she stretched her fat limbs and she flipped through the pages of a trashy novel, while the Jew in the tallis sketched drawings.

Loda's mother gave her Benjamin Franklin's for the Golden Coral restaurant buffet, and her and her Jew in a ladle went there. The courses of macaroni and cheese were artery clogging and the sweet tooth in the

Jew's gums standing at the soda pop machine broke the glass on the floor. He was wearing green sandals and short brown pants with a tee shirt with the ladle-shaped hat. She stared at the plate and said, "Fine," and feeling a sting, the Jew lifted his sandaled foot on the table with a big chunk of glass sticking out of his big toe. He said, "Tashlik."

The green sandal in the sink flopped with red blood on the toe and the glass slid out with ease. The primary colors swimming in the sink, the Jew in the ladle-hat prays with silent wordless thoughts. Goldy with the long, golden hair was three chairs between him and Michael. There was milk spilled on Michael's desk and dripped on the carpet, and she was smiling because the boy with Jew's hair was staring, and suddenly, began crying stifling cold tears.

"Help me with this?" Romaine asks the Jew in the tallis.

The Jew in the tallis and Romaine take the bones from soft-boiled baby chickens, peeling the skin with the thumb and forefinger swimming in the hot fluids. The grease rubs in the poultry and with pinching fingers tare the meat off the bones, tossing the bones in the oily bucket. The pretty girls with hard hoofs on the slippery tiles wet with water slide on the drain, and looking behind the pots, the Jew in the tallis glances out the kitchens' window facing the tables in the dining area at the apron girls with filly legs. There is a bowl with romaine lettuce in vinaigrette.

"Don't toss that!" Romaine says.

The phone rings with Romaine's wife dialing from Cameroun. She calls mostly after the boss and the waitresses have clocked out. They have been separate for months while he studies in Baltimore and have a daughter. The girls in the bakery with subtle steps, and to a man shut in a square with no getting out, the sickness is dangerous. The Jew in the tallis' health slowly was suffering for months, and before the fever set in, he was told in confidence by Max the baker that he was deeply in love with a girl. The blood disease Loda had in her circulation was caught by the baker and he was suffering whereas the Jew was clean. There was flooding in New Orleans and the entire city drowned. The night before on the news pictures from the flood flashed on the television screen so he took an evening constitutional in the dark; walking hungrily, he was conversing with his stomach and gall bladder floating in the outside air along the neighborhood. His organs were drifting from his clothes. In the hospital were nurses injecting morphine and portioning blood from his veins. The walk he took the night before was the candy bride and groom on the wedding cake in the marriage celebration of pancreas and liver; his gall bladder was dissected from his abdomen. In no time flat he was out complete in anesthesia dreaming of the encounter with the doctors with clipboards, his signature and he believed he was talking with ghosts around the operating table. He was in an Elysian landscape having an interview with Tom Brokaw about New Orleans and the terrorist attacks on 9/11. He could not speak because there was a tube in his mouth, breathing in place for his lungs while under the injection. The news moves so fast.

Step 10

In the digestive system were the three branches of Government, the gall bladder is the executive branches thick bile. Gallstones clogged the bile pushing from the gall bladder, which the liver had to jury over, was certainly the judicial branch because of the processing of toxins and liquids. The laws absorb the moist poisons of the liver organ in the human corpus and the liver was being eaten by the executive gall. The stomach is the legislative branch as it digests slowly. The most reliable of the organs and the least likely for something wrong to have began to grow inside. Stomach fluids wash acids over enzymes as liquids enter the blood through digestion. For four months he was holding his stomach like a pregnant woman as the muscles in his back inflame birthing pangs.

The anesthesia with the morphine injection formed a synthesis in his brain of a dragon heralding advice while two armies feuded over the lives of his lover and associate. Single-strand, fatty foods were taboo and there were numerous restrictions on walking, driving, sleeping and heavy lifting. The dragon had smoke steaming from its smoking nostrils. The Jew, Isaac was sketching the nurses in the hospital moving around the hospital bed while he was asleep, remembering the time he was out in a bar drinking and the couple sitting to his side kissing on a bar stool with the whites of his eyes inking a drawing of the great bald man and the small, Jewish woman; curving her neck to his lips, her hair falling over her shoulders over her eyes, his nose arching over her chin and lips, they fade out the corner his white pupils dilating stare at the ceiling in a sweaty nausea; he sketches the gray faces at the bar with two morose women losing their hair thinning as the palate on his ink brush. The ceiling thick with dark purple and gray paint swirls in the golden dark room as the band tunes. Crackers crumble on the mahogany as liquor brightly glows with mirrors reflecting green lights and the bartender stands behind the wooden bar upset by the crowd absent from drinking. The rest is a jig-saw puzzle the Jew in the tallis pieces together fragments in the sheets on the stiff hospital bed.

Ike says, "I'm not thinking of anything. I hear the telephone ringing. I want red wine but that will only make things ring louder."

"Want to pay? To leave?" the Jewish woman asks.

"I don't like to talk about that deficit: Bupkes," Isaac says, mispronouncing the old Yiddish word for having nothing.

Loda hears talking from across the room, where a woman writhes snake-like on the floor. He is standing with his shoulders like a man trapped inside a suitcase with the arms and legs bent crosswise. He has the ticket.

"Kronnenberg," Loda says to the bartender.

Max the baker is standing and measuring the fluids in his balance organ, as the room seems to bend with the tuning. The face of Hieronymus Bosch appears briefly and vanishes in the crowd swaying with the ceiling fixtures. The snake politely farts.

"My throat is parched and sore," Max says. Max mumbles no one can hear. He eyes a snake wearily while he avoids the eyes of the hunger. "I miss her," Isaac says to the bottle snakes.

The conversation has already spilled out into the halls and Loda barrages words. "I drink like a snail," Loda says. He says, "Can I get you a drink? My hands are steady but not quite still. Can you roll a kosher one?"

"New York Nickel?"

"I have no way of paying if filing for bankruptcy, have no possessions to claim, also there is nothing for the loan collectors to take if I have nothing," Isaac explains why he cannot pay. The guitar is on stage shivering and has a pale grimace and reeks of cigarettes. The bodies twist and writhe in the shadowy room as the bassist hits the E vibrating the lowest tone when the finger presses the string before striking a tall tone, although the musicians rarely meet. The drum rattles the snares, the guitar strums and the crowd lingers posing in the stillness. The lights turn dark and the figures are silhouettes.

Isaac moves eerily through the darkness to the folding white curtains to the bathroom. He holds his penis in his hands and urinates while he unconsciously in midstream hums and almost sings out from his guts O sol mi. He shakes off imagining he has just passed a kidney stone. The salty urine swirls down the bowl submarine bubbling acidly. He feels his balls heavy as lead and big as pinecones yanking his pants and staring at the fading writing on the walls: decide how to live marrying beautifully, living happily, drinking well, eating well and pissing purely. He stumbles out of the bathroom through the curtains into the spaces as the vibration of strings lulls the audience into a doze. Romaine says, night, tiredly collapsing over the floor because there is no one in the bathroom. Listening to the band, he stares wondering the distances his voice spreads through wires and out the ways, echoes on the streets, resounding. He's contemplative with wet eyes and hungry breath. There is anger in gestures such as nervous twitching, neck, nose scratching and eyes dark. The lights switch on; the figures writhe and twist; a voice cries from the halls, "See what monsters you become! See how hideous we all are!"

There was a pain in his lower abdomen shot through his neck and spine that became the first shock in Isaac's life to give up drinking and resulted in the surgeon removing his gall bladder through tubes, the second was weeks after eating breakfast his pancreas became inflamed causing pain. In the hospital, he was prohibited from ingesting solids and was nourished through the IV in his right hand. Morphine made his head lighter like he was swimming. After were huge doses following the pain; he was having medication that lasted and seemed to last.

"I have to apologize," Ike said to the nurse, "this was an accident but the IV needle slipped out of my hand when I was getting up from bed. That's the numeral Roman four also. There was a lot of blood spill on the blankets. I can get up in the morning."

"Why do you say that?" the nurse asked,

"I was saying it is four in the morning, I have been waiting for the nurse four minutes, it's just a coincidence and it was not my intention, it was an accident," he says with a scar beneath his left eye from a cat's claw.

"I have a three year old daughter," the nurse said, "I also enjoy playing on the flute."

"Have you heard of Eric Dolphy," Isaac asked, "Mingus?"

"No, I have a friend in the symphony that knows," she said as she put the IV in. Even under the drugs, he could tell she was gently humoring his sensibilities, doubting what sense he had left after the operation. The names of people he knew were faded in recollection of the week. He doubts whether he remembered the event at the bar enough, although wasn't terribly important. Life after the surgery would now be different than he had, and there were certain things he'd have to give up. He wanted to know if there were things that would take the place of missing if anything was going to change, except those that he knew.

In the morning he woke up with pain from the incision in his chest where blood was let to relieve pressure on his abdomen. The IV monitor was plugged in the wall to the right of bed. He was watching the television confirmation hearings of John Roberts to the Supreme Court feeling light-headed because the morphine was faded. Switching channel on the television was simple though the remote only moved the dial upward on the switchboard. The news had Hurricane in New Orleans; North Carolina. The nurse came in to check his temperature and read his charts. The nursery for newborn children in the medical ward was on a different floor yet the expression in the young nurses bright blue eyes spoke differently than he thought as impotently a dead body in the hospital. He felt like a dead man. The nurse shot him morphine.

"You have to shower today," said the nurse, "and to do that you have to stand in the bathroom, stand up in bed and take a walk over the floors in the bathroom, sit on the chair and scrub your teeth, sponge off your arms and legs."

He felt like a child being told to bathe, a limp baby in the arms of a tired, young nurse. The breakfast brought gelatin, crackers and orange juice. He beneath the table over his legs cracker crumbs. He would have liked to ask her for milk before she left the patient ward. Later that day she brought him flowers sent from people at the kitchen where he labored. They're beautiful yellow dandelions, tulips and orange hyacinths for a long time, he sleepily smelled the flowers in strange daydream over in the bed on his side; he was instructed to get up out of bed to lift up his side onto the bed and the tiles.

"Walk," she said, and he did.

The flowers were lying on the table for his afternoon nap with their petals spread beside a lovely letter he was writing. He pondered the day before he went to the hospital after he had had the first attacks of the illness. He was writhing on the carpet in the most agony he had ever felt. After the stretch of several hours, he collapsed on the mattress in his room to sleep before waking fine in the afternoon and calling sick into work. He was healthy for two days before collapsing in agony on the third day in the morning, riding in an ambulance to the ER and signing for a prolonged stay in the hospital. He lived with a delusion of hope and went working, drank, gobbled much food as he would on the night before collapsing, and he took a long walk in the neighborhood at dusk.

His sides were hurting and he had to sit on a park bench around the neighborhood housing development. The houses were nice brick models with a large, clean-cut, grassy lawn around the buildings with trees for shade in the bright months. Isaac did not see the houses because he was looking across street. He was not looking at crabtrees. He was in his own and was what was going on and the shade in the moonlight was awfully troubling to see. There was a young lady that sat to his side on the bench; he could not turn to see her because of the pain in his side. He could tell she was looking at him and he found this pleasant.

The muse of his inspiration was a beautiful prose, "the gentle moonlight beneath the shade of the bark caresses the smooth bumps on your cheek. I have not the pleasure of knowing your name; maple leaves, shadow; the distinct smell of your voice with the breathing of your sighs on the edge around my neck muscles, sincerely, I.S."

"This is a beautiful night," she said to Isaac.

"I love you," he whispered.

This was confusing to her because it was impulsive. The green, the trees on the shadows swaying on the walk smothered the warmth of the summer lights on warm bodies. He was not bothered by the FDA, nor in the militia, doesn't know the terrible strange weapons of war in our time, yet the thought of cherry blossoms in the Japanese spring was fresh in his dreams, her smell sweet in the way; he did not notice that he was sweating.

"You seem worried," she said.

"I have to take a trip soon," he said, "and will maybe never see you again; if I'm fortunate, you will hear from me."

"Are you leaving?" she asked.

"This is the last day before I leave in the morning," he said, "and cannot tell you where I am going because…"

That next morning he phoned the hospital for an ambulance and that girl strange did not see his return home. The letter written in a trance was never given an address or a name for the destination made it in the trash. Flowers smell sweet as the days go passed in the hospital, the water evaporates and the flowers rot in the glass vase. Isaac recovered from his surgery and lives with his illness prohibited from drinking and on a new diet. There are loose memories never born: "This was a picture of myself" in the prose. He wrote, "blue eyes and stark, handsome chin carved in masculine frame. I have dark hair and my mouth and lips are clean shaved, as you might remember me with a beard and I no longer have. Tall, skinny with stitches in my right stomach; I have circles under my wet eyes because have lost sleep."

There is a pain that seems to last after the medicine has worn. He was so pale in the morning before leaving the hospital then his red, afterwards. The cause for his suffering was elusive; if no cause were found, it would make so much more sense than where he woke up. He blames the service. He blames the sickness.

In the morning, Ike had become used to rising with the dawn and the chattering of the blue bird that lived outside his window in the tree, it seemed strange to be having pains. He got out of bed and stretched his arms, his penis dangling in the air out of his boxer shorts. At work he stumbled slouching over the kitchen sink and scrubbed at grimy schmaltz on greasy pans. He was having a conversation with his sore hand crying over a pool of whirlpool suds. The soap chemicals ethylene poly-chloride permanent dry stung his nose and the smell of bleach flushed his lungs. The radio station played softly Kovalevsky Cello Suite as the food prep cut tomato and eggplant with the knock of knives on the wood doe-shaping table. Water from the sink pipes leaked on the floors.

Step 11

Clipping toenails on the washtub with nail clippers, the Jew in the tallis day dreamed the Lithuanian nanny with the file used to trim his nails, and he used to chew his toes with his ivory, chipped teeth. He had dirty nails and the dirt tasted hard with sharp, cold spats, and someone sang with an alto tenor, the songs gypsies sing to children with healthy, glowing cheeks. The cruising on the Potomac with the oars rowing in the canoe with the stern on the flat lake, the oars sinking deep with the waters' flow pushing hard against the bow while the grey clouds drizzle, the lake quickly bubbling with rain and Isaac paddling hard with Romaine towards a forested island. The wind chill cutting in soft fatty biceps, the boat docking in the mud lifted off the lakeshore. The thunder cracked.

In the mossy bricks in the square terrace behind the row house, the Jew boy, five year old, touches the loose bricks. The bricks let loose, and the muddy insects squirm in the paved earth. The centipedes squiggle with a thousand legs, and the maggoty larvae with gray shells roll in symmetrical ovals with legs tucked underneath. The ants scatter in chaotic quibbles. The giant in the sky, the red brick in the masonry slips in the niche touching the rough, red clay. The scattered grasses with blades waving in the wind sprout in the herb garden thyme, sage and aerate dry cologne. The vegetable gardens in the Sowebo neighborhood are tall grasses with fledgling trees, fences with tomato vines taller than the youngest; an overgrown jungle in the light quibbles the caretakers in the row houses farming vegetables in the dawn. Tying tight the rope to the boat on the lakeshore, Isaac and Romaine carry the canoe with the slack like a child in a swinging hammock. The burning rope in Ike's fingers ignite the delicate knots he tied the tomato vines to the fences with, loosely so as not to bruise but hold the tomato's ripe bodies. Romaine and Isaac hike on the forested island with the bright flashes of lightning touching on the lakes unflinching water, and the wet rain falling through the thin branches. The vacationers duck in the mud with the light showing on a damp hill and the trees swaying in the storm.

"Lightning strikes the tallest things and those in motion," Romaine shouts, "those trees!" The April storm subsides and the vacationers walk to retrieve the boat, paddling away on the lake, staring in the deep green seaweed the endless depth, microscopic organisms, breathing in the anaerobic, phosphorescent light squiggles. The motorcycle revving engine on the hard steel accelerator with the driver in a plastic helmet with the shaded visor reflecting the UV rays. The clear highway driving in the cool exhaust, the Yankee father driving west to see his Iroquois daughter, where years counted in the trailing smoke with the caustic oils, gasoline and rusty metal stored in the garage behind Loda's house. The Jew in the tallis in a lawn chair, a red wine bottle cork cut out with a switch blade, and Loda with her auburn curls sipping Beaujolais while the old man was away.

In the blurry evenings Loda's Sunday dinner where the drinks mingled in sparkling glass chimes with the drinks. The unwelcome silence between the bells chiming while the cold knife cut the thirsty chicken, the juice spilling, and after the dinner her Uncle Tom's jests and the other guests play charades and drink Scotch, Loda walking off with the Jew in the tallis taking a romp in the bushes, spilling his seed in her. The highway bends and seems to lift the bike off the road, and the driver seems lifted in the sky thrust off the pavement like a canoe paddling on the water.

The evening with the lavender sunset on the stoop with the porch light on, waning yellow on the soft sunken eyes waiting for Max the baker driving there, the fat, black boy Danny from down the street came there with a surprised look. "Is Loda there?" he asks, and just as the Jew in the tallis says yes, the baker's car drove up and Loda came from behind the house with an evening dress. "You can sit here and wait," he says, "because I was just leaving," and Max the baker curses behind the steering wheel in the car.

"You're leaving her there with that guy?" Max says as the car was driving away. "Did you see he was staring at her?"

"He's just stopping there, and he's an old friend of hers, besides," the Jew in the tallis says, "she's a good lover."

The uncomfortable silence on the porch was blasted with the stereo in the Sedan; Max the baker turned on with the Jew in the tallis tilted his beard at the stars in the pale glass. The awkward drive because a 'good' lover was not all he meant to express and the dress she wore carrying with her was not falling naturally at her heels. The brown hues with floral patterns in silks brushing against her smooth goose flesh, square the sharp curves on her body with the Sedan taking sharp turns; the designs she wears are not the stars, marijuana smoke trailing out the cracked windows weakening the day.

The crack in the asphalt jumped the cars' bouncing rubber tires and the Sedan swerved at a burlap sack in the street with something moving inside. There was a thump and the Jew in the tallis was sweating ferociously with the smoke. "What was that?" Max asks, and they drive around the block in South Baltimore North of the Trucker's.

"We hit a cat," the Jew in the tallis says. "He's dead."

The row houses' flapping wire door squealed, slapped close with a metallic click and the bakers' assistant with the baker crashed on the couch staring at the television. The news was flashing 'Shorty' the killer on death row, the lethal injection on the table tempting a bright, dull opaque death. The lazy three-legged cat was hopping on the rug, old waiting for a comfortable sleep with the blaring TV. The Jew in the tallis staring in blurry lenses, eyes glazing over listening to the chewing, swallowing Max's jaws, "The dog ate the beef," Max says. "He ripped the plastic wrap off the beef in the refrigerator raw, and he's sick!"

The Jew in the tallis was picturing the cows' slaughtering with the blood on the knife, the food served in truck stops letting piercing cries as the flesh hits the stove. Max's head seemed to float on his body, and he was thinking something; looking at the shelves with Poe, Shakespeare in gold leaf black smoke blowing in the air. "Are you thinking about the circus clowns?"

The strange Christmas holidays in the fascist old man's house with the camera on Loda's bedroom curtains was confounded when on dawn's crack, a van with circus clowns with arms akimbo carried the intoxicated, old man on his lawn, and laid his body there. The Jew in the tallis was a witness to the scene, and Max's.

"What? No," Max says, "Get out' of here nigguh!" The Jew in the tallis walks off with Max's floating head haunting severed with hairs waving course and sharp bone teeth carved like sticks whittled in sharp points. The path on the fenced yard was dark with shadows on the brick row houses sharply pressed in dull lines. Max's severed floating head was laughing with the bloody maw dripping with cows' blood, the sharp piercing howl of the dog.

"Get out here, nigguh!" the Jew in the tallis shouts in the wire. The square hat like the state hovered on his head with the strings dangling from the stars, Max's severed head floating out of the row house with his angry teeth. Max's curly beard and reddish curls on his trimmed head.

"I braided hair for young chicks," Max says, "so the Jews' hairs are braided." He was a hard worker, as the saying is, work is work. The Sedan is sleek black leaning against the curb on the hill, the baker and the Jew in the tallis walk after the barking dogs. The bad weed smoking green smoke with the radio blaring from the car saying Congress debates the slaughter of the Armenians by the Ottoman Turks as Genocide.

"Pussy, pussy, pussy," Romaine says a cat call with his arms brushing against the backs, Max's head floating with his beard tilted at the sidewalk and glowing eyes. He reaches in the car and turns the knob on the radio counter-clockwise. The sidewalk bends beneath mouse steps padding on leathery shoes. Andy's was on the second floor Michelangelo's above the pizza house. The stairs leading up there were beside a bell ringer, and the walk hardly fractured the heart beats. Romaine's steps are the hardest, knocking the loudest, the legs on the others are strong like a horses' clop.

"Hey," Andy says, "what are you doing here?" The charge through the portico was met with Andy's fat cats, and there were three hoods huddled by the glass.

"We're out to find Max's sick dog!" the Jew in the tallis says. The television was stuck on an episode with Al Bundy's show.

"Isn't that the guy that murdered all those women, it?" Max says, "Is, that's Ted Bundy!" Romaine and the Jew in the tallis park like Ted Bundy's Tan Volvo Station wagon on the sofa. The bulge in his pants, wallet with condoms, greenbacks and his drivers' license was sat on with the obese cat. Isaac pats the cat with his right and lets the left hang on the sofa; the hoods are splitting cash and smoking crack. The low bending ceilings close in, water damage from the loose shingles on the roof and a dog barks in the street, heard outside the window with the blue moon hardly lighting. The brush moustache with hair hanging in his eyes in a cloud of smoke, etches a pale drawing with dark hair, icy blue eyes wearing a wool cap folded, cats' purring in the Jew's lap, the television scans the closing credits as the Jew in the tallis lifts the cat off the rug, "Goodbye!"

"The fumes," the Jew explains, "are making me cough!"

"The gas chamber in here," Max says. "We better find the dog because he's sick and we work opener tomorrow!" The television credits flash starring Ed O'Neill as Al Bundy in white letters on the closing scene; Al sitting on the couch staring at the TV with his hands on his jock strap. The jock counts the Jackson's laughing noticeably with teeth showing molars pushing on his cheeks. He's wearing a Colts' jersey 19 in blue with white letters and the folds are larger than he is.

"Ethanol," the Jew in the tallis explains, "the washing machines use ethanol fuels, alcohol fumes in the breathing air." Romaine is an Orioles baseball fan, so he's already out there before the closing credits read. The bakery shift workers are dog hunters tonight and clop on the steps with a fast charge pacing the sidewalks. "Hey Johnny," the hood asks with the fronted image men have when the police have had cause to search, "Shorty is getting the gas?"

"Lethal Injection," Johnny says, 19, the Colt's quarterback long, long ago. "No one gets the electric chair, it's all very humane."

"You are not tall enough to get fingered in a lineup," Andy says, "Shorty is."

"Don't believe he is," the folded wool cap says.

The dogs chase in the streets with howling behind fences, and the breeds in rough growls, shrill cries are reflected clouded as the mirror on a mud puddle. Splashing in gutters with muddy paws, the wet leather shoes leave trails on the grass on the hill sliding down to the train tracks where the train does not ride the rails. The rusty iron tracks clang a muffled ring with the hard clops. The clustered trees grow on the tracks. The leaves flutter in the trees where the birds nest at night, and the cats are sheltered indoors with the frightening dogs bark scaring pussy cats. The highway cars whistle on the overpass miles behind Andy's. Storage warehouses are rectangular, stone statues on solid pavement. The truck drivers move cargo with road mammals. "There are no fences," Romaine says, "and the storage garage is deserted." He tosses the marijuana cigarette in a heap beside the trash littered on the ground beside the compactor. The storage building's unlocked with the back way unhinged slightly with a wooden ramp wedged beneath the frame. An iron winding steps on the gray concrete walls ascend the side of the building, the iron ringing with the footsteps on the rise. The blanketed stars concave on the flat roof, standing with his eyes closed, the tallis balancing on his head, the Jew falls flat. Max's floating head balancing on his pink neck perched on his shoulders; lifts the Jew. Romaine helps with his arms akimbo leading the dog hunter's to the ledge on the roof, "Hurrah Armenians!"

The trucks are so small on the surface, the satellite on the roof transmits radio waves great distances; the trucks briefly commune here, as bees in hives; the flashing lights in the dark alert the dog hunters. There are sirens. Isaac stands with his legs arched wide stupefied, "those police sirens?" he asks, "we did not trip an alarm, and no one knows we are here." There is a loud bang with a sulfurous aroma with an acrid tinge blowing in the air, Isaac stares sickly over the ledge in the dark. Romaine runs short strides on the hard top short steps, Max's severed head swerving, and the dog hunters taste the harsh smoke rising in the unhinged lock. Falling on the fire escape's iron stairs spiraling hypnotically with the Isaac sick out of sink; the smoke presses against the windows, the building; the stones heat with fury; the dog hunters chase the sound of barking in the trees where the tracks are. Max's dog barks at the smoke rising from the flames, limply on all fours with red teeth and a fat stomach hanging on the train rails. His matted brown fur is bristly like porcupines' quills, the dog leans whimpering on sore legs. Max cradles the dog on the walk home, and half-way to Max's Romaine says, "See you later!" Max's goodbyes are the last he says when the Jew in the tallis walks west from the south houses where the streets bend in a triangle, the turn where the burlap sack with the tire tracks on the street lays limp, he nudges with his toes, the soft, dead flesh on the hind legs, and the smaller bipedal arms. "Oh, it's a rat!"

Isaac tosses the keys on the table, the inch thick door closes and the nightmare is on the marble stoop. He recites the evening prayer, hangs his hat on a rack; nods at the passing cat as he walks the narrow stairs. He lays in bed staring at the ceiling in the attic, before dreaming the fragments on the sidewalk, glass, windshields hammered with the cracked desires sizzling in a cracks' pipe. The banana board, a yellow skateboard turns with the rider's weight; he was eight years old riding uphill on his stomach with his head lowered at shimmering glass sparkles on the sidewalk, crack smokers broke the cars' windshields, with the banana board bending on the wheels. The Jew boy leans around the corner at the street behind the houses where money becomes hands with crack. The haggard faces are no longer frightening when at night, laying awake in bed in the dark; there is scratching beneath the mattress, and lifting the mattress as turning a paper stack, a deadly rat paws under the bed bars hissing with sharp tongues. The Ouija board with the lens translating the words ghosts whisper in the dark, the Jew boy traces. Goldy's fingers on the dial, the letters trace, 'I S I C.'

"Isaac?" Goldy says, and the Jew boy gasps, "Me?"

The afternoon in the square with the picnic blanket on the hill, the Jew boy tackles her while she has a muffin in her hand. He wrestles with her on the red checkered blanket with soft flesh pressed together in a sugary doe. The hard and soft pounds press when from over the hill, the sun shines on the green grass while the picnickers rolling on the mounds spilling her golden hair. The hard dirt he has pressed against her.

Johnny has the needle doses with heroine and passes the gun to her, that she presses into her arm vein. Laying lackluster on the sofa bed, she falls in a coma and close to sunrise someone presses tablets in her mouth, P's. "Here," he says, and her thanks are slowing breaths, halting her pulse. Goldy is laid to rest.

"I quit!" Isaac tells his boss the next morning, and Max is riding off the hard night by the trash cans smoking a cigarette. Stepping on the porch in the brisk night air with the row houses across the street on fire, twenty-one years before hiring at the Bakery and quitting three months later, the fire trucks line the streets. Tall poles with dulcimer hammers are swung on the rooftops with strong firefighters holding the handles, shattering glass thick as sugarcane. The boy walks with bare feet on the hot tar roofs in the sun, wandering on the ledge with tiny strides. The slanted roofs bend over the back alleys and the cats leap with bending knees across the gap between the houses. In his underwear crouched at the people moving below, he can see for blocks the stray leads. The heat pressing hot tar on the balms of his feet, there is a flash like rain drops a shiny metallic ball presses through the temple on an African, the red blood on his forehead imitating fascists, angled like the last Lithuanian Jew shot in the camps.

The glass falls like dollops of chard. "Murderers," the Jew boy says, the fire rushing through the floors like children's faces pressed against a fence bending the wires to snap. The smoke rising over their bodies with black, deadly coils suffocating the children breaking against the wires. The fences' rattle in a crib in the hands with cracks' snapping the coils on a gas, the fire spreads the curtains, the drapes and the shoddy rug.

"Nobody lives there," a neighbor says. Firemen shattering windows; roaring glass in the smoke curtains scratches the cornea on the boy in the smoke. The fire starter is hiding on the second story folded like a fetal pig. The hydrants siphoned water and the hoses were heavy as pythons. The brick flames raging with the water brushing against the building with a water spout poured endlessly never filling the corridors.

The bakers' oven hot, red stone surface with a crawl space large enough for rising bread, and a head taller so the loaves don't touch the oven. Six months later, Isaac asks for the old job back, where months earlier Max has crawled in the oven in the night, writing in the flames with his blood running hot, and in the morning, the early shift workers pulled out a dry husk.

Step 12

The milk in the refrigerator is a few days past the expiration date and smell sour, Isaac sniffs with his nose. The sourness is expressed in his eyes and pouted lips, and Loda's grandmother stares vacantly with an obtuse awareness. She is wrinkled and her brain's smooth surface is fractured with a misfiring wires crossed in her longevity. The sour milk has been left out, and she looks sad. Her grocery shopping lists exclude the milk and she is always careful to notice the expiration dates, the poison ugly face stickers stuck on medications and the photographs presented to her in an album.

"I always smell the milk," Isaac says. The precaution stems from his French teachers' warning, stay wary of the first signs your olfactory's fading, because brain tumors are nullifying your senses. She is drawing a list on a paper envelope with red crayon; the design with scarred letters resembles a burning house; her allowance to prepare meals with no supervision arouses some suspicion from Isaac, whom she believes is her son some days. Those are the bad days. Her son is there with the groceries arguing with her on the balcony and says the phrase kill her with a whining falsetto, the last Isaac hears with Loda sitting on the stairs sobbing as he stomps with loud stomps. Daisies she had planted in the trampled grass sob in a menagerie shadows cast from unripe fruits with limber cherry's bending crisp bark. Isaac is reading the lists with injured senses; she hugs his shoulders from behind the kitchen chair where grandmother and he break short fragments in sentences; she leads him with her hands on his hairless palms in the sitting room where for quick sex they make love on the couch. Grandmother converses with troubled thoughts in her brain. The aging woman has wrinkled ripples hard as the bark on her flesh's grooves like a dried apricot. Her neck is a narrow, elongated stalk with a polyp forming that stares with wild grey hairs brushed neatly from her face; her breasts are nipples with long scars where the cancer has been cut beneath her armpits; the loose belly fat leans against her uterus. The tumor grows big as a grapefruit for three months, and she tells no one until the milk grows sour because the one thing she remembers late when the sniffed milk is bad, she needs to write her lists.

"What of Loda?" Loda's grandmother asks. "I will take care of her," Isaac says, "you have no worries," but he knows she has the mark of death on her where the tumor has grown. The cancerous fruit is cut from her loins and the chemotherapy racks on her autumn with recklessness, when bending over in the night she vomits over the bed's shoulders while the Jew sleeps with Loda's frail, fetal shape in his grapevine embrace, staring helplessly across the hall in the unhinged nest. There are birds nesting in the cherry tree.

The autumn weather strips the tree's limbs and the cherries are cut from the branches, while her sick grandmother sleeps the autumn lovers walk in the shadows the marble monument streaks in the downtown. The dark rustic houses are brick, painted green, trees planted on stone stoops on gray while the lovers' walk is on hot asphalt where arabbers wheel horse-drawn carts shout holler, holler, holler in black tenors at the pedestrians and home owners until the arabbers throats get sore.

"Watermelon, get melons red to the rind, lady," the arabber says.

"Apples," Isaac says, "red ones." His lover picks at the fruit on the cart in her fingers pinching the ripe skins. The oranges bubble fiery with round grapefruits on red apples, crescent-shaped bananas, green plantains and yellow, star-shaped fruits on the cart's ledge. The horses' muscular hind legs stomp hardened on the street rocks with handles pulling at the varnished wood. The wheels in large, round tracks totter as the arabber handles a bushel with apples.

The street opens in the cross-shaped park with a general riding on his steed on the steep hill beneath the Washington Monument, where kids climb the stairs with condoms full with water and drop the balloons from the top, splashing on the bus stop where people wait for the traffic to move. The baby colts' halt in the stables in southwest Baltimore where the arabbers house the horses, horses' hoofs resting on grass, snorting hot noses, shaking manes with mantles that fall on loose shoulders, unhitched to a wagon to drag fruits in the hot sun with the cold, the moon and night in the skies. Here, older horses hanging with a saddened mull as the houses are not where they belong, and are told to leave with a stern swipe of a stick the housing authorities shake.

Isaac cuts a slice from an apple and left the bushel in the bottom of the refrigerator to ferment. There is a green Chrysler in the street with the lights on, windows open and leather interior a light tan. Romaine is at the watering hole waiting for Ike like horses on stools sitting in stalls with the bar between bending backs with long snouts and noses stuck in the beers, staring at the green glass behind the bartenders while resting on fat cushions where the bottles balance along the ledge. A bald man with a blue shirt, the front arms with strong hands are palms face down on the bar. He sniffs whiskey, bobs listening to the songs playing. "If a bottle fell from the ledge, there would be a sharp glass shard, almost like a knife," Isaac wonders watching from the outside.

"Adler's arm theory, the older brother always stronger than the young, the older wrestles the younger down, I can see," Isaac says as he drags the bald man with a swift kick to the stools' legs, "That you are younger, and you think me old!"

Ike pulls from his coat and stabs in his shoulder above his lungs, where he squirms and falls on the bar floor. "Hey!" the bald man shouts. "You lawyer!"

"You call me a lawyer!" Isaac says, "And here in your coat if you let me use your cell phone, to get an ambulance so you don't die!"

The beer spills slightly as the stool sitters turn to see, and the cut is so minor, he leaves upset with no recourse. The cigarettes smoke leaves clouds above the glass bottles with the distorted reflection in the glass showing a twisted expression. Ike believed the bald man was the man who killed Goldy, like the horses pounding days with hoofs, wishing that that just Judge's gavel hammers. The guilty man is irreproachable.

They drive Isaac's Sedan to the hills of California, grape country in the north farms with San Francisco a day's drive, staying in Hotel 8's and 6's with gasoline at the lowest cents to the gallon with Romaine, and his wife. The week long trip lasts for several weeks with drinking, smoking ten cent weed with tobacco, the taste seasoning the apartment with a thick aroma. Adobo, Romaine calls the aroma, which is a Latino seasoning with garlic, oregano and other Latino spices with a sauce for pork, poultry or fish cooked in vinegar. He has a striking chiseled chin, closely shaved with a straight razor, fuzzy hair cut short, black as an apartment with the lights off. With the lights on, a green haze permeates the windows closed looking out at the pitch black darkness. "Did she die?" Romaine asks, while his wife sits with legs out in a dark ebony dress with long locks tied in bows, with gentle nudges urges her husband to tell Isaac to pay a loan he has indebted after months paying no rent, drugs, food and gasoline.

"She fought the good fight," Isaac says, prolonging the grandmothers' sickness with his embellishments. He sees there is no skimping the costs for his travels, selling the Sedan as collateral to his friends, he buys a plane ticket home with the surplus.

"The train doesn't ride there much anymore," Sarah says. The singing sound of hammer pounding train tracks resound in her hallucinations, a residue of the *Chattanooga Chow-Chow* song, "*'bout a quarter to four, read a magazine and then you're in Baltimore*," she sings slightly weightless. The younger nights, desperately scrounging for drinks, drinking methanol with the stove hot to keep the warmth in, Sarah came stumbling in and to Isaacs dumb blindness, she pours the antidote, Ipecac; he stares blindly at the green fields below the gaping curvature the plane traces from flying an accrue pendulum landing in the dark purple night. The ground appears so far, there are things he cannot see in the gray, writes poems for her on paper with blue ink.

The door is open, and I'm waiting
On the stairs
I go downstairs, but the door is closed,
And I'm waiting on the stairs.
I'm waiting.

I could go there and dig you up
Outside
Your golden hair, your daffodil
Eyes
The dirt thumps on my little cart

I'm pedaling.   Roses aren't selling
For just pennies above cost
And the cars are honking
like geese

I'm standing on the stairs
and the cops are taking me
away

About the author

Zachary Crabtree was born in **SoWeBo** (**So**uth **We**st **B**altimore) house with wood floors, brick walls, tall ceilings, a skylight and a marble stoop. He came to be a writer because all the books collect overflow in cardboard boxes. He's got long-playing microgroove records.

He moved to live with his grandma and Zadie's Frank Lloyd Wright home in Chattanooga, Tennessee. The song *Chattanooga Choo Choo* pretty much says it all*, "You leave the Pennsylvania Station 'bout a quarter to four / Read a magazine and then you're in Baltimore"*

Other great titles from:

www.BurningBulbPublishing.com

Available at www.BurningBulbPublishing.com
or scan the QR code to learn more on amazon.com.

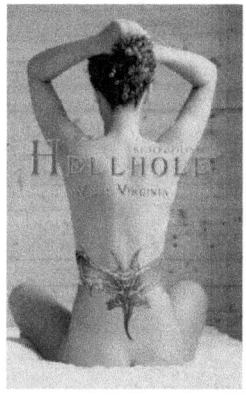

Available at www.BurningBulbPublishing.com
or scan the QR code to learn more on amazon.com.

Available at www.BurningBulbPublishing.com
or scan the QR code to learn more on amazon.com.

www.ingramcontent.com/pod-product-compliance
Lightning Source LLC
Chambersburg PA
CBHW071251130626
46556CB00003B/1266